"Why Do You Want My Baby, Virginia?" He Asked.

She twisted a long strand of hair around her finger and walked a bit closer to him. Clad only in her negligee, she appeared so small and vulnerable, yet every inch a sexy woman. He knew she'd seduced him for a reason, but right now with only the faint lights from the bedroom and balcony illuminating the room, she seemed ethereal.

But he didn't want to trust the vulnerability he saw in her. She'd lied to him.

"It's all tied to the curse. Your family and mine are connected."

"Interesting. Do you honestly think having my child will break the curse?"

"Yes. But I don't think we can fall in love."

"That's not going to be an issue," Marco replied. "I'm not going to fall in love with you."

Dear Reader,

The MORETTI'S LEGACY trilogy idea came to me out of my fascination with my Italian grandmother's superstitious nature. She was a devout Catholic, but also believed you could curse someone or put the "evil eye" on them. That blend always intrigued me, and a few years ago, I found a book called *Italian Witchcraft* that talked about the old ways…and when I say old, I mean from times of Roman rule.

My idea was simply a cursed family. The curse was simple: The Moretti men would either be lucky in love or in business but never in both.

Cassia Festa put the curse on Lorenzo Moretti. He broke her heart when he chose car racing over her, and she wanted to make very sure that he never found love in another's arms. To be fair, Lorenzo probably would not have ever fallen in love because he was too enamored of racing and his dreams of building a car empire.

This story takes place around the globe in the glamorous world of Formula One Racing. I love to travel, and the idea of having a job that takes you to every continent in the world (as Grand Prix drivers do) is one that makes me envious. This story blends together a lot of things that are important to me: family, tradition and the idea of taking the seeds of the past and sowing them into a brighter future.

I hope you will enjoy this journey into *The Moretti Heir,* the first story in the MORETTI'S LEGACY miniseries.

Take care,

Katherine Garbera

THE MORETTI HEIR

KATHERINE GARBERA

Silhouette®

Desire

Published by Silhouette Books

America's Publisher of Contemporary Romance

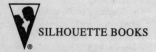

SILHOUETTE BOOKS

ISBN-13: 978-0-373-76927-8
ISBN-10: 0-373-76927-X

Recycling programs
for this product may
not exist in your area.

THE MORETTI HEIR

Visit Silhouette Books at www.eHarlequin.com

Printed in U.S.A.

Books by Katherine Garbera

Silhouette Desire

KATHERINE GARBERA

is a strong believer in happily-ever-after. She's written more than thirty-five books and has been nominated for *Romantic Times BOOKreviews* Career Achievement Award in Series Fantasy and Series Adventure. Her books have appeared on the Waldenbooks/Borders bestseller list for series romance and on the *USA TODAY* extended bestsellers list. Visit Katherine on the Web at www.katherinegarbera.com.

This book is dedicated to my son…beautiful face.
Who could not love a boy who is so full of fun
and laughter, quick wit and intelligence?
Thanks for all the silly conversations,
tickling matches and just spending time with me.

Acknowledgment:

Thanks as always to my wonderful editor
Natashya Wilson.

One

Marco Moretti, by anyone's standards, was a man who had it all. His win today was part of his plan to become the most decorated Moretti driver of all time. His grandfather Lorenzo had won three back-to-back Grand Prix championships—something that Marco had done, as well, but this year he intended to surpass that record.

Both Moretti drivers were tied with three other drivers for the most Grand Prix championship wins, but this year Marco would win a fourth, something he had craved from the time he was a rookie driver.

He had no doubt that he would do it. He'd never failed at anything he put his mind to, and this would be no different. Why, then, did he feel bored and restless?

His teammate, Keke Heckler, was sitting at the banquette next to him, drinking and talking to Elena Hamilton, a *Sports Illustrated* cover model. Keke looked as if he had the world in his hands. All Marco could think was that there should be more to life than racing, winning and partying.

Oh, hell, maybe he was getting sick, coming down with a cold or something.

Or perhaps it was the family curse. Supposedly no Moretti male could succeed in both business and love.

"Marco?" Keke asked in his heavy German accent.

"Yes?"

"Elena asked if Allie was meeting you here later," Keke said.

"No. We're not together anymore."

"Oh, I'm sorry," Elena said.

A few minutes later, Keke and Elena left the table to go dance and Marco sat back against the leather seat and watched the crowd. This party was as much for him as it was for the jet set that followed the Formula One races. He saw other drivers mixed in with the sea of beautiful women, but he made no move to join anyone.

Allie and he had drifted apart during the off-season. It was as if she wanted him only when he was in the spotlight. A part of him craved the quiet life. He couldn't give up the glamour that came with racing, but sometimes when he was alone he wanted someone with whom he could share the quiet times of his life. A companion at the villa in Naples where he retreated to be an average man.

He glanced around the room. None of the gorgeous women stood out—they all were too beautiful for words, but he'd never find a woman here who wanted that type of lifestyle.

What was wrong with him?

He was poised to usher in a new era for Moretti Motors. He and his brothers had grown up in an odd world of wealth and privilege, all the while knowing that they had no riches of their own. Something that he, Dominic and Antonio had changed as soon as they were old enough.

The three of them were now men who commanded respect in the cutthroat business world of automotive design. Under their guidance, Moretti Motors had returned as the leader of the pack for exotic cars. The power of the Moretti engine and the state-of-the-art body design combined to make their cars the fastest in the world, something that Marco was aware of each time he got behind the wheel of his Formula One race car. What more could he want?

His breath caught as he noticed a woman across the room. She was tall—probably almost five-nine, and had hair the color of ebony. Her skin was pale, like moonlight on the Mediterranean. Her eyes... well, it was too far for him to be certain, but they seemed deep and limitless as he gazed at her across the room.

She wore a subtly sexy dress, in the same sky-blue color as his racing uniform. Her hair was caught up and a few curls hung down, framing her face.

Marco slid around the booth to stand up. He was used to letting women come to him, but he needed to meet this woman. Had to find out who she was and claim her as his own.

As he stood up and took two steps toward her, she turned away, disappearing into the crowd. His heart raced as he started after her. But a hand on his arm stopped him.

He turned to see his older brother, Dominic. They were of a height, and both had the same classic Roman features—at least, according to *Capital,* an Italian business magazine. Something that Antonio, their middle brother, liked to tease them about.

"Not now," Marco said, intent on finding the mystery woman.

"Yes, now. It's urgent. Antonio has just arrived and we have to talk." Dominic was very much the leader of their fraternity. Not just because he was the head of the company, but also because he was the engineer of this new wave of prosperity for Moretti Motors.

"Can't it wait? I just won the first race of the season, Dom. I think I'm entitled to one night's cele-bration."

"You can celebrate later. This won't take long."

Marco glanced back to where the woman had been, but there was no trace of her. She was gone. Maybe he'd imagined her.

"What's up, and where is Antonio?"

"On his way. Let's go to the VIP section to talk. I don't trust this crowd."

Marco wasn't surprised. Dom took no chances when it came to Moretti Motors. He'd been the one to realize that the curse put on their grandfather, Lorenzo, when he was a young man was responsible for their parents losing their wealth. Marco didn't put much stock in curses made by old Italian witches, but his father believed the curse was responsible for their family's change in fortune.

When they were teenagers, he and his brothers had taken a blood oath never to fall in love. They vowed to restore the glory and power of the Moretti name.

Marco and Dom made their way through the crowd to the velvet-rope section of the room. Marco was stopped many times by well-wishers congratulating him on his victory, but he kept looking for that dark-haired woman. He didn't find her. They reached the VIP section and found a quiet area toward the back of the room. It was walled in on three sides and had a curtain for privacy.

Antonio was waiting there for them. "Took you long enough."

"Marco is the champion. Everyone wants a piece of him tonight," Dom said.

"What is the problem?" Marco asked, not interested in having one of their brotherly discussions that led nowhere.

"The problem is the Vallerio family is adamant that we can't use their name on the new production car."

The Vallerio was Moretti Motors' signature car and had been out of production since the sixties. Bringing the model back was Dominic's plan to firmly reestablish their dominance in the marketplace.

"How can I help?" Marco asked. "Keke or I can take the stock car to Le Mans and win the Twenty-Four Hours with it."

"Impossible. Their lawyer sent a cease and desist letter to us."

"We need to get to the Vallerio family and convince them to let us use the name," Dominic said.

"What do we know about them?" Marco asked, his interest in the dark-haired woman momentarily abated. He knew how important it was that Moretti Motors go ahead with their plans.

"That Pierre Henri Vallerio hated Nonno and is probably jumping for joy in the afterworld at the thought that his descendants have something we need," Antonio said.

"So a family feud…"

"Of a sort. I think they'd say no just to prove they can," Dom said.

"Well, then, I will have to offer them something they can't refuse," Antonio said.

"Like what?" Marco asked. His middle brother was used to winning. Hell, they all were.

"I'll figure it out," Antonio said. "Leave this one to me."

"We can't let this derail us," Dom said.

"We won't," Antonio said.

And Marco knew it wouldn't be a problem for long. The Vallerio's lawyer would be surprised when he had to deal with Antonio.

Virginia Festa had had a moment's panic when Marco left his seat and started walking toward her. She knew enough about him to realize that he liked his women interested, but not obvious. So she turned away hoping…oh, hell, she had turned away due to panic.

Melbourne, Australia, was steamy in March— something that she had anticipated before she'd left her home on Long Island. In fact, she'd planned every detail of this trip with excruciating precision, knowing that timing was everything. But she hadn't anticipated the human element. A mistake she was sure her grandmother had made, as well, when she'd placed the curse on the Moretti men.

She suspected that her grandmother—who had only a rudimentary knowledge of the ancient *strega* witchcraft—hadn't realized that when she'd cursed her lover, Lorenzo Moretti, and his family she was also cursing the Festa women. Virginia had spent a lifetime studying the curse her grandmother had used, trying to unravel the words so she could break it. There was no way to just take the curse back, since her grandmother had been the one who'd spoken the words and she was now deceased.

It totally ticked her off that she had panicked after coming this far. She was putting into action the plan she'd been thinking about since she was sixteen, since the moment she'd discovered the curse her grandmother had placed on the Moretti men and, by accident, the Festa women.

She wiped her damp hands on her classic Chanel gown. She was going to have to try to find Marco again—find him and charm him without giving away her plan. The key was to be vague. She had spent hours studying books on the *strega* spell her grandmother had used to curse the Morettis and looking for a way to break it. She'd determined through her research that to put the plan in action, she had to be anonymous.

She had only her grandmother's memory of the words she'd spoken—words that Cassia had written in her journal and that Virginia had studied. Her grandmother had demanded retribution for her own broken heart, and in doing so, she'd doomed the Festa women to always have broken hearts.

There could be no joining of Festa and Moretti hearts. They had to stay forever apart. But their blood… As she'd studied curses, Virginia found a loophole. Separately, both families were doomed forever. But a child of Festa and Moretti blood could break the curse. A child given to her freely from a Moretti would repay the broken heart her grandmother had received from Lorenzo Moretti two generations ago and lift the curse on the Morettis and the Festas.

Now that the moment was here, she was really nervous. It was one thing to sit in her condo and make plans to seduce a man. It was something else entirely to actually fly around the world and put the plan into action.

She stepped out of the crowded room and onto the terrace that overlooked downtown Melbourne. Until now, the places she'd seen had been only the small town in Italy where her grandmother had grown up and her own home on Long Island.

Tonight, standing on this terrace looking out at the black sky dotted with stars, she felt like she was on the edge of starting something new. All the *strega* magic that her mother and grandmother had taught her had its basis in being outside. She looked up at the moon shining brightly down on her and took strength from it.

"It is a beautiful night, is it not?"

The deep, masculine voice sent a tingle down her spine and she wasn't surprised when she turned around and saw Marco Moretti standing there.

The panic she'd felt inside the party didn't return. Instead, as she looked over her shoulder at him, she felt a sense of power come over her.

"Yes it is," she said.

"May I join you?"

She nodded.

"I'm Marco Moretti."

"I know," she said. "Congratulations on winning today."

"That's what I do, *mi' angela*," he said, grinning at her.

"I'm not your angel," she said, though she loved the sound of him speaking in his native language.

"Tell me your name and I shall call you by it."

"Virginia," she said, very aware that her last name would give her away. So she kept it to herself.

"Virginia…very pretty. What are you doing here in Melbourne?"

"Watching you win," she said.

He laughed out loud, the sound washing over her senses like the warm breeze that stirred around them.

"Will you join me for a drink?"

"Only if we can stay out here," she said. She didn't want to go back into the craziness of the party. Out here, she felt in control and better able to concentrate. Plus, she needed all the *strega* magic she could summon. The night sky filled with stars and the bright moon would help her.

"Certainly," he said. He signaled one of the uniformed waiters and they placed their drink orders.

Once their drinks came, Marco took her elbow and led her farther away from the people lingering on the terrace. The terrace spanned the entire side of the building, and as they walked along, she became very aware of his hand on her arm, of the subtle brush of his fingers over her flesh.

When they reached a quiet area with no one around, he stopped walking and dropped her arm. Leaning back against the railing, he looked at her, his dark brown eyes intense. She wondered what he saw, she hoped she seemed mysterious, sexy, sultry. She was afraid she was going to give up the game she was playing by betraying her nervousness.

"Tell me about yourself, *mi'angela bella*," he said.

She hadn't counted on her senses being engaged by Marco. She'd figured she'd come here, flash some leg and a hint of cleavage, and that he'd be turned on and take her to bed and she'd leave in the morning.

Instead she found that she liked listening to his voice. She loved his accent and the rhythm of his words as he spoke. Liked also the scent of his cologne, and the way that he made her feel like she was the only woman in the world. And of course, that fit what she'd learned about him—that his relationships, while short-lived, were very intense.

"What do you want to know, *mi diavolo bello?*"

He laughed again and she understood why he was considered so charming. Charm imbued every part of him. "So you think I am handsome?"

"I think you're a devil," she said.

"I love the sound of my native tongue on your lips," he said. "Tell me about yourself in Italian."

"I only know a few phrases," she said, "What is it you want to know about me?"

"Everything," he said.

She shook her head. "That would be a very boring tale. Nothing like the famed story of the Marco Moretti."

"I bet that's not true. What do you do?" he asked.

"Right now I'm on sabbatical," she said, which was the truth. She had taken six months off from her teaching job at a small liberal arts college to follow the Formula One racing season and meet Marco.

"Why?"

"I'm going to be thirty next year and I decided it was time to see the world. I've always wanted to travel but never had the time."

"So it's just a happy coincidence that we are both in Melbourne?"

"Yes," she said. A very happy coincidence, put in play by her own actions.

"Melbourne's only the first stop. This is one of my favorite cities."

"What do you like about it?" she asked. She knew little about the man beyond what she'd read on the Internet and in magazines.

"Tonight, I like that you and I are both here."

She shook her head. "That's a corny line."

"It's not a line, but the truth," he said. "Come and dance with me."

She took a sip of her Bellini. She'd caught his attention, diverted the conversation away from herself, and now… "Okay."

"Did you really have to think it over?" he asked, taking her hand in his and drawing her near to him.

"Not really. I just wasn't expecting this."

"Expecting what?"

"To find you so attractive."

He laughed. "Good. I wasn't expecting you, either, Virginia."

"What were you expecting?" she asked.

"Another victory party where everyone pretends that they are happy for me, but no one really cares."

"Is that usually a problem for you?"

"Not really. That's just the way this crowd is. Everyone is here to see and be seen."

His words revealed more than she was sure he intended them to. But before she could ask any more questions, he leaned in, cupped her face and brought his mouth down to hers.

The scent of his Scotch was sweet as he parted her lips with his own. She felt the warmth of his breath and then the gentle brush of his tongue against her mouth.

And in that moment she knew—*strega* magic or not—this was a dangerous mission she'd set for herself. Because not falling for the charming Marco Moretti was going to be harder than she'd ever imagined it would be.

Two

Virginia's plan was working…a little too well. Marco was smooth and charming. She'd expected that. But he was also very funny and a bit self-deprecating.

Everyone wanted a piece of him tonight. A moment to bask in his glory. He had the aura of someone who was going to break that record on wins in the Formula One circuit, and everyone wanted to be close to him.

Since they'd come in from the terrace, she tried to leave a few times, not being comfortable in the spotlight. But he kept her by his side, his fingers linked loosely with hers as they moved through the crowd.

She didn't have to try to be mysterious here. No one knew her, and to be honest, she didn't think anyone wanted to know her tonight. She was simply a pretty woman hanging on Marco's arm.

The feminist in her was a bit outraged to be delegated to nothing more than arm candy.

"I am sorry, *mi' angela,* but winning always means that my time is not my own."

"It's okay," she said. She was learning a lot about Marco from watching him. She wondered if her grandmother had realized what the Formula One lifestyle was like. Was this why Lorenzo Moretti hadn't wanted to settle down with her grandmother? Maybe having experienced the high life, he hadn't been ready to give it up for home and family.

"What are you thinking, *cara mia?*"

"I'm thinking that you can't remember my name so you keep calling me by endearments."

"Virginia, you wound me."

"Doubtful."

He smiled. "I do want to know what you are thinking. You look too serious for a woman at a party."

She didn't know how to respond to that. She wanted—no, *needed*—to be mysterious. She couldn't allow herself to forget for one moment that she wasn't here to fall in love with Marco Moretti. She was here to break a curse.

But when he pulled her into his arms on the dance floor, she forgot about plans and curses. She forgot about everything except the way his arms felt wrapped around her. The way his shoulder was the perfect place to rest her head, which she did for only one second, because the sexy scent of his aftershave was too potent that close.

"I was thinking that at this party, everyone wants something from you."

"Including you?"

Yes, she thought, but didn't say it out loud.

"It's okay, I know you do. Everyone wants something, I want something from you."

"What do you want from me?"

"Another kiss."

Of course he did, and that made her agenda so much easier because she wanted him to want her. But at the same time...

"You're doing it again," he whispered into her ear. "I'm going to think that you aren't happy to be with me."

Shivers ran down the length of her body from her neck to her toes. Her breasts felt heavier all of a sudden, and her nipples perked up, as if they wanted the warmth of his breath against them.

"Of course I'm happy to be with you, Marco. You are the man every woman wants...all you have to do is beckon and any woman here would come to you."

"I don't want any other woman tonight, Virginia, only you."

"Why?" she asked.

"I could say that it is the hint of mystery in those

deep, chocolate-brown eyes of yours. Or the smooth-ness of your skin against my hand."

"But that's not it?"

"No, *cara mia*, it's not. The reason I want only you is much more base and too demanding to be tamed by words."

"Lust."

"You say it with disdain, but there is a power to lust and to attraction at first sight. From the moment I caught sight of you, I have been unable to think of anyone else."

She smiled up at him and let go of those silly girlish dreams she'd secretly harbored about love. Lust was exactly what she wanted from Marco, and she should be very happy that he felt it.

"It's the same for me."

"Is it?" he asked, drawing his hand down her back. Her skin was exposed by the plunging V at the back of her dress and his fingers felt big and warm against her skin.

He pulled her closer to his body as he spun them around the dance floor. His mouth touched the ex-posed skin at the nape of her neck. His lips felt warm and moist against her skin as he said something she couldn't understand. All she understood at this moment was that she wanted Marco Moretti.

Her flesh was sensitized to him. She felt alive in this man's arms. Perhaps it was the magic of the night, or maybe it was the peach Bellinis she'd drank going to her head. But deep inside her, where she kept the superstitious part of her soul, she knew it was the curse coming out. She knew this attraction went beyond her and Marco.

It was something cosmic and wonderful, she knew. Especially when he lowered his head to hers. She didn't wait for him to kiss her, but instead rose on her tiptoes and met his mouth with her own.

He brushed his lips over hers before opening them the slightest bit. She felt first the barest rush of his breath over her sensitive lips and then the smooth taste of his tongue.

He kissed her with the kind of passion she'd only read about in books and seen on movie screens. She clung to his shoulders as everything feminine inside of her responded to everything masculine in him.

Kissing Virginia was addictive. Like the rush he got from going over two hundred miles per hour on the track. There was that feeling of being in charge of something he knew he couldn't really control.

Her mouth was sweet and she clung to him like she couldn't get enough of him, either. He maneuvered her off the dance floor, keeping one arm around her waist and tucking her close to his side.

"Where are we going?" she asked. Her voice was breathless and her lips, swollen. There was something almost ethereal about her. He would never have admitted that fact out loud, but having grown up under a very suspicious Italian mother, he believed strongly in things that couldn't be explained.

"To a place where we can be alone. Is that okay

with you?" he asked her. Expectation sizzled in the air between them. He felt almost as if they'd met before. With her, he didn't feel the distance that he felt with most women, as if they had an expectation of something that he couldn't deliver on.

She nodded and smiled. Her mouth was wide and so damned sensuous. He'd never get enough of kissing her. And for tonight, he didn't have to. He ran his hand down the center of her bare back, enjoying the feel of her soft flesh under his fingers.

"I'd like that," she said. There was a hint of shyness in her voice, a timidity at odds with the brazen and mysterious woman he'd known her to be so far.

"Virginia?"

"Yes?"

"Are you sure?"

He saw hesitation in her eyes, but then she nodded her head, curls dancing around her face as she stepped forward. She rose on tiptoes and drew his head toward hers and brushed her lips over his. She kissed him deeply and passionately, arousing him with just that one aggressive move.

"I'm very sure," she said.

"Good," he said, his own voice sounding husky.

He led the way out of the party toward the elevator and almost groaned when he saw Dominic coming. He didn't want to talk to his brother now.

"Merda," he muttered under his breath.

"Excuse me?" Virginia said pulling away from him. "Is everything okay?"

"Pardon me. My brother is heading this way, and with him there is always a discussion about business."

He fought the urge to hit the call button for the elevator again. That would make it look as if he were afraid of Dominic, and that wasn't the case. He just wanted to get Virginia out of the party to be alone with her.

That made him feel a bit odd. He'd never been one of those men who needed to keep a woman all to himself. With Virginia, he realized he wanted just that.

"I didn't realize that a driver would be involved in the running of a company," she said.

"At Moretti Motors we have decided to keep things all in the family. So that means that we all take an active role in running it."

"Doesn't that interfere with your driving?" she asked.

Marco liked being involved in running the company. Dominic, Antonio and he had decided the reason their father had lost his controlling share of the company was that he had not been involved in the day-to-day details. And that was one thing he and his brothers were determined not to let happen.

"Not most of the time…but it can put a crimp in my love life."

She rolled her eyes at that. "Saying things like *that* might be more of a problem for you."

Marco shook his head and gave her a charming smile. The same smile she'd seen when he'd graced the cover of *Sports Illustrated* last year. "Most women don't mind."

"I'm not so sure about that," she said.

"I make up for my…how do you say…ill manners in other ways that women appreciate."

"What ways?"

"I'll show you as soon as we get out of here."

"I'm going to hold you to that," she said. "Should I leave you alone with your brother?"

"No," he said, not wanting her to disappear again. "Dom won't be long."

"Marco, do you have a minute?" Dominic said as he reached them.

Marco tucked Virginia's hand in the crook of his arm, keeping her close to his side.

"Not really. I promised to show Virginia one of my favorite places in Melbourne. I can meet with you tomorrow to discuss the matter," Marco said.

Dominic didn't look pleased, but then his brother rarely did. "That will be fine. But I'm flying back to Italy tomorrow, so my schedule is tight."

"I understand," Marco said. As much as he resented the delay in leaving with Virginia, Moretti Motors was as important to him as it was to Dom.

"Virginia, let me introduce you to my oldest brother, Dominic. Dom, this is Virginia…." He didn't know her last name, he realized. This wouldn't be the first time that he had a one-night stand with a woman whose last name was a mystery to him. So why did it bother him?

"*Affascinato,*" Dominic said.

"The pleasure is mine," she said.

"Did you enjoy the race today?" he asked.

"I missed it," she said, blushing.

Marco found that odd. Most of the women who followed the circuit never missed a race. He looked down at her. "You did?"

"My flight was late. I was upset, but I had this party to look forward to."

"Where are you from?" Dominic asked.

"The United States," she said.

"Most Americans prefer NASCAR racing. Do you follow that sport, as well?" Marco asked, realizing that with his brother here he was learning more about her than he had all evening, talking to her.

"No. I've always been in love with the glamour of Formula One."

He raised one eyebrow at her. "What do you think is glamorous about it?"

"This party, for one," she said. "Oh, look, the elevator is here."

The doors opened and Marco wondered at her vague answers. Was she hiding something? She wrapped an arm around his waist and squeezed him closer to her. "You did promise to show me your favorite sight in Melbourne."

"Indeed I did. *Ciao*, Dom."

"*Arrivederci*, Marco."

Virginia didn't say much as they got in Marco's sports coupe convertible. She recognized it as a Moretti model. The car was pure luxury on the inside and all speed under the hood. She'd never feel confident enough to drive a car like this, but Marco handled it like the professional driver he was.

As they left the hotel behind he glanced over at her. "So you're from the States?"

She'd known he was going to ask questions. She'd done a good job of keeping her past vague and the spotlight on him, but the conversation with Dominic had probably made him realize how little he knew about her.

"Yes. Long Island. Where did you grow up? I know Moretti Motors is based in Milan, but do you live there?"

"I have a villa in Milan, and my family has an estate outside of the city."

"Do you like living in Milan? I've never visited there," she said. She was very aware of the Moretti family estate in San Giuliano Milanese. Her grandmother had gone there to curse Lorenzo, and there was a faded picture of the Moretti estate hanging on

her wall back home. Her grandmother had be-
queathed it to her along with her journal.

"It's a fashionable city and there is always something to do there." He shrugged as he glanced over
at her. "It's home."

She envied him the feeling of belonging in Milan.
It was there in his voice and his words. Unlike she,
who'd never fit in anywhere, he had a place that he
called home. And that was a big part of why she was
determined to break the curse her grandmother had
placed on them by accident. She wanted—no,
craved a home and a family. She was tired of always
being alone. Her mother and grandmother were both
deceased, and no matter how hard she tried, the
bonds of family seemed to always be just out of her
reach.

Having his child would give her a chance at happiness. A chance at that elusive dream she'd longed
for. Once she broke the curse, she would marry and
give her child a father and siblings.

"We're here." Marco' s words startled her from
her thought.

She glanced out the window as a uniformed valet
came to open her door. The high-rise building was
a monument to modern architecture, its lines distinc-
tive and clean.

"Good evening, Mr. Moretti."

"Good evening, Mitchell."

Marco led the way into the foyer and to a bank
of elevators.

"I thought you were taking me to see your favorite
spot in Melbourne."

"I am. My penthouse has a spectacular view of the city. It's amazing," he said, glancing down at his titanium watch. "In about two hours, the sun will come up and you will be amazed at how beautiful the sunrise is here."

"Will I?"

"Yes, I think you will," he said. "Unless you'd rather I take you back to your hotel."

She shook her head.

The elevator arrived and they entered. They were alone in the marble-floored car, and as soon as the door closed Marco entered a code on the keypad and the elevator started to move. He drew her into his arms and lowered his head, kissing her.

She felt the return of the passion he'd evoked in her on the dance floor. Her body longed for his. She'd missed his touch during the twenty-minute drive, and she wondered how much of this feeling was due to the magic spell she'd cast earlier to help her break the curse. She wasn't a practicing witch, but she figured she'd better enlist as much help as she could before she came to Melbourne. How much of it was due to the fact that she needed him to be obsessed with her?

And how much, if any of it, was real?

When the doors opened, he broke the kiss and ran his hand down her bare arm, linking their fingers together. She squeezed her hand against his and followed him eagerly into the foyer of his home.

"I have this entire floor. Would you like a drink?"

"That would be nice," she said.

He led the way into the living room. There were floor-to-ceiling windows that lined the wall and a sliding door that opened onto a huge balcony. Marco kept one hand on the small of her back as they walked across the room.

She felt a slight bit of panic as she realized this was it. She was going to sleep with this man, whom she'd known for less than five hours, and then she was going to walk away. It was what she'd planned for more months than she could count, but now that the moment was here…

She stopped in the middle of his living room as a surreal feeling swamped her. She was aroused, every inch of her skin sensitized from his kisses and touch. As she glanced at the Monet painting hanging on one wall and felt the thick Arabian carpet under her feet, she knew she was really here, that this wasn't something she was imagining. Yet, at the same time…

"Would you like to step outside? We can sit in the hot tub and have that drink."

She glanced at Marco, with his strong Roman features, and saw in him the glimpse of her future. She wasn't going to let panic or doubt swamp her, and give up everything she'd ever wanted.

She needed Marco Moretti, and it seemed that he wanted her tonight. And that was all she needed. She repeated that in her head as she stepped out onto the balcony and let the warm air wrap around her.

Three

Marco poured a glass of champagne for each of them. He wasn't inept when it came to taking care of the women in his life, despite the fact that Allie had often complained he paid no attention to her. The fact was, he was careful to pay only a certain amount of attention.

He was careful not to let his emotions get involved, always leery of falling for a woman and thereby ruining his life.

His mobile rang and he cursed out loud as he saw from the caller ID that it was Dominic.

"What do you need now?" he asked in Italian.

"Just wanted to remind you to be careful with

Virginia. We can't risk anyone falling in love, especially now."

"Mordalo," he said to his brother.

"I'm not jerking your chain, Marco. You know that falling for a girl isn't something we can do."

He glanced across his penthouse apartment to the balcony where he could see Virginia leaning against the railing. She didn't *look* dangerous. He saw nothing in the woman to indicate she could bring about the downfall of Moretti Motors.

"She's just a woman, Dom," he said, even as, deep inside, a part of him protested. But the truth was, his priorities were simple—racing and winning. Moretti Motors and then enjoying life. And Virginia was a woman who would make his life very enjoyable tonight.

"Make sure you remember that."

"I always do. I think you're afraid that Antonio and I are too much like you."

There was silence from his usually loquacious brother. Dom had fallen in love in college, and that one, brief lapse in his vigilance served as a constant reminder to Dom that all women had the potential to tempt any of the Moretti men.

"I don't know what I fear. Just be careful, Marco. This is the year that everything will change. We have worked hard to get to this point. We are launching the revamped Vallerio model. You will surpass the Gran Prix record for most wins…."

"I am aware of that. *Buona notte,* Dom."

"*Buona notte,* Marco."

He hung up the phone, thinking of his oldest brother. Antonio often complained that Dominic needed to get laid so that the old boy would relax. But Marco suspected that Dominic's heart was the most vulnerable of all of the Moretti men.

"Marco?"

"Coming, *mi' angela.*"

A warm, gentle breeze stirred the air around the balcony as he approached Virginia. Her hair lifted in the wind and for a minute it seemed as if she were part of the night. As if this was the only place she could exist. Almost as if she were a fantasy. But she was a flesh-and-blood woman, as he'd ascertained by kissing her and holding her in his arms.

"I thought you'd changed your mind," she said.

"Not at all. I just wanted to make sure I had everything perfect," he said, handing her the glass of chilled champagne.

"Is this part of the charm you promised to show me earlier?"

"Do you think it is?"

She laughed, and the sound was like music on the wind. He closed his eyes and let the worries that his brother always reminded him of disappear. For tonight he was nothing more than a winning driver with a beautiful woman.

"I'm not so sure."

He arched one eyebrow at her. "What will it take to convince you?"

"I'm reserving judgment until morning."

He handed her the champagne flute, which she took.

"To your victory on the track today," she said.

He tapped the lip of his glass against hers. *"Grazie."*

He kept eye contact with her as he took a sip of the sparkling wine.

"To mysteriously beautiful women," he said, lifting his glass toward her.

"Grazie," she said with a shy smile. "But I'm not beautiful."

"Let me look again," he said.

She stood still, a hesitant, almost fragile smile on her face as he stared at her features. Her wide brown eyes seemed luminous and filled with secrets. The thick eyelashes that surrounded them and the light dash of makeup on her lids made them look exotic.

Her high cheekbones and creamy skin were next. He lifted his free hand and traced the line of her brow and then down the side of her face. Her nose was thin and long, marking the elegance of her face, but it was her mouth that entranced him.

Her upper lip was a bit fuller than the bottom one, and both were rosy red and so soft to his touch. He ran his thumb over her mouth, tracing the bow at the top and then stroking her bottom lip.

"I see nothing to change my opinion," he said.

"Maybe in your eyes I'm beautiful, but I promise you other men don't see me that way," she said.

"The eyes of other men don't matter, *mio dolce.*"

"No, they don't…I just…I've never done this be-fore," she said suddenly, her words coming out in a rush.

"Come back to a man's apartment?" he asked, unable to help feeling a bit honored and possessive of the fact that he was the first man she'd felt this strongly attracted to.

And he couldn't deny the attraction between them. He hoped she'd never know how much he wanted her and how much power that gave her over him. He needed her in ways he was only beginning to realize.

"Yes…I'm a bit nervous."

"It's not too late to leave. We can finish our drinks and I can take you back to your hotel."

Virginia realized that Marco was making very sure she couldn't say he coerced her into anything. Or perhaps he was just being a gentleman. What did it say about her that her first thought was that he was protecting himself?

But there was little he could do to protect himself against her. She wanted nothing more than this night in his arms—and his sperm.

She felt cold and calculating, thinking the words. She knew that every night millions of people had one-night stands and it meant nothing.

But she didn't. She had been pretty sheltered all of her life. After being told early on that love and romance were not in the cards for her, she'd become determined to find a way to make her romantic dreams come true.

She knew that her motivation for being here was breaking the Moretti curse. But when he'd described her just a moment ago, talked about a beauty she just couldn't see when she looked in a mirror, she felt as if this encounter meant more than she knew.

She felt as if Marco wasn't just the means to an end. That he wasn't just another victim of a long ago, bitter love feud between their families…felt as if he could be the man who would make her fall in love with him.

And love for Festa women wasn't a good thing.

"Virginia?"

She shook her head to clear it. Glanced up at the moon and gathered the strength she needed to forget about consequences and right and wrong. For this one night, she wanted to just enjoy the moment with this man.

"I'm not leaving," she said.

He smiled at her, and she realized just what true male beauty was. It was his smile when he looked at her.

"Are we going to just stand here and wait for sunrise?" she asked.

"Not at all. I thought we could sit in the hot tub and relax. Enjoy the champagne and the rest of the evening."

The warmth of his hand on the center of her back

and the low thrum of the hot tub located on the end of the balcony settled her nerves. She let go of all the planning and concentrated on the fact that she was here with a charming and sexy man.

"I'd like that," she said.

"There's a changing room over there stocked with robes," Marco said, his voice deep and dark in the moonlit night. He gestured to the small building next to the tub.

Having spent most of her adult life waiting for this exact moment, she knew it was time for her to act. But action was the one thing that had always scared her. Her grandmother had loved Lorenzo Moretti and that single act had completely ruined Cassia's life.

Perhaps sensing her unease, Marco said, "Do you know about the stars?"

"What?"

"The stories of the different stars and why the constellations fill the sky," he said. Wrapping his arm around her waist, he led her to a double lounge chair and gestured for her to sit down.

She did, and Marco sat down next to her. He put his arm around her shoulder and shifted until she was lying next to him with her head on his shoulder.

She looked at him and knew without a doubt that he had sensed her keyed-up nerves. And she wondered if this was a sign from the universe that she should give up on her plan. Was there a side effect she'd missed when she'd determined the way to break the curse on their families was by getting pregnant with Marco's child?

"The sky is different here," Marco said. "In the Northern Hemisphere, where we both live, you can never see the Southern Cross."

She stopped worrying about seduction and relaxed against him. "I had heard that. Where is the Southern Cross?"

He pointed at the sky. "Right there…do you see it?"

Her gaze followed the line of his arm, and she saw four stars in a diamond shape in the sky. The Southern Cross. "Does it have a legend with it, like Orion or Sirius?"

"Not really. Because it is visible only from the Southern Hemisphere, we have no Greek or Roman legends associated with it."

"What is that constellation?" she asked pointing to another one.

"That is Leo. Egyptian priests used to be able to predict when the Nile would flood based on its position in the sky."

He talked about other constellations and she began to see beyond the international celebrity race car driver to the man beneath. He was used to moving in a world of privilege and wealth, yet tonight he was just a man.

"How did you become interested in stars?"

"My father. He isn't into racing or cars…not the way a Moretti should be." He turned on the lounge chair so that he was leaning over her. "But he loves legends and the past…he has spent a lot of his life reading about stories of old."

"Where are your parents now?"

"In San Giuliano Milanese. It's where our family home is."

"Are you close to your parents?" she asked.

"In some ways. I've always shared a love of the night sky with my father. When I was younger, most of my time alone with him was spent outside at night, looking through the lens of his telescope."

Being an only child, she'd had too much time alone with her mother, who had been very sad most of the time.

"Why didn't your father like cars?" she asked. She knew that Giovanni Moretti was rumored to have been too easygoing to run the big automotive company. That he wasn't interested in business… only in making love to his wife.

"He liked them, he just loved my mother more. So business didn't hold his interest."

"Yet, it does hold yours," she said.

"Tonight I can see why my father was distracted," Marco said.

She thought she saw surprise in his eyes as he revealed that, but he recovered quickly, leaning in close to kiss her. His kiss was soft and slow, one of seduction rather than full-out passion.

He swept his hand down the side of her body, unerringly finding the zipper in the side of her dress.

Instead of unfastening it, he simply traced his finger over the seam.

His mouth moved along her jawline with small, nibbling kisses, then dipped lower to caress the length of her neck. She shifted in his arms, trying to bring her body into full contact with his as he continued to tease her.

Her breasts felt sensitive and the skin of her arm beaded with goose bumps as he continued to move his hand over her body. She wanted more.

Marco had always had an innate gift for seducing women. Dom had suggested it was because he was Italian and wooing women had been bred into him, but Marco thought it was more than that. He'd never been callous in his seductions and he'd walked away from women who he knew would regret having made love to him when they woke in the morning.

But he couldn't walk away from Virginia. He surprised himself with the depth of the need he had for her. Still, if he made this about the physical, then his emotions would recede and she would be nothing more than a passionate memory for him to look back on, years from now.

The rich darkness of her hair contrasted with the creamy whiteness of her skin. He drew down the zipper at the side of her body and watched as the sky-blue material gaped open. He slipped his hand under the fabric and touched her skin.

Her breath caught and she shifted in his arms, turning on her side so they were now facing each other. He reached between them and drew her hands up to the first button on his shirt.

Staring into her wide, chocolate-colored eyes, he saw the shyness that was so much a part of her melt away as her fingers brushed against his chest.

Blood rushed through his veins, pooling in his groin and hardening him as she started unbuttoning his shirt. Her fingers were cool against his skin as she worked her way down his body. When she finished unbuttoning the shirt she pushed it open and he shrugged out of it.

He growled when she leaned forward to brush kisses against his chest. Her lips were soft and not shy as she explored his torso, and he felt the edge of her teeth graze his pecs.

He watched her, his eyes narrowing and his pants feeling damned uncomfortable. Her tongue darted out and brushed his nipple. He canted his hips forward and put his hand on the back of her head, urging her to stay where she was.

"Where did you get this?" she asked, one finger tracing over the scar under his left nipple.

"Tony pushed me out of the fig tree in the backyard when I was eight and I landed on a hoe that the gardener had left lying on the ground."

"Did it hurt?" she asked. She braced one hand on his chest as she leaned over him.

He shifted under her and lifted her in his arms so

that she straddled him. He leaned up and kissed her lips. "At the time it hurt very much."

"I'm sorry," she said, leaning down to lave the spot with her tongue. "I have a scar, too."

"Where?" he asked.

She blushed and then shrugged her shoulders, pulling her right arm out of the dress. The bodice loosened and the other sleeve slid down her left arm until the dress pooled at her waist. She wore those strapless bra cups that were clear in color. He could see all of her breasts and yet as he reached up to touch them, he felt only fabric and not the sweetness of her flesh.

"The scar isn't on my boobs," she said, with a little laugh.

"No?"

"No," she said. "It's here."

She pointed to her right side an inch below her breasts. It was long, almost two inches, and had faded with time.

"How did you get this?" he asked, stroking a finger down the length of it. She shivered in his arms and rocked against him. His erection twitched against her core.

"Trying to climb into the window of our house. My mom locked the keys inside."

"I'm sorry," he said. He lifted his hips to tip her body toward him. He found the scar with his lips and rubbed his hands over her naked back, enjoying the feel of this warm woman in his arms.

She put her hands on his shoulders and eased her way down his chest. She traced the muscles of his abdomen and then slowly made her way lower. He could feel his heartbeat in his erection and he knew he was going to lose control if he didn't slow things down.

But another part of him wanted to just sit back and let her have her way with him. When she reached the edge of his pants, she stopped and glanced up his body to his face.

Her hand brushed over his straining length. He removed the bra she still wore and then lifted her up so that her nipples brushed his chest.

"Hmm…that feels so good," she said.

"Does it?"

"Yes."

Blood roared in his ears. He was so hard, so full right now that he needed to be inside of her body. But he had to take care of details first.

"*Cara mia,* I hate to ask this, but are you on the pill?"

She pulled back for a second. "I'm…yes."

"You are taking the pill?" he asked.

She nodded. "And I don't have anything else you need to worry about. What about you?"

"I'm clean."

"Good," she said.

He pulled her closer and kissed her until she relaxed. Then, impatient with the fabric of her dress, he shoved it up to her waist. He caressed her creamy thighs. God, she was soft. She moaned as he neared her center and then sighed when he brushed his fingertips across the crotch of her panties.

The lace was warm and wet. He slipped one finger under the material and hesitated for a second, looking up into her eyes.

They were heavy-lidded. She bit down on her lower lip and he felt the minute movements of her hips as she tried to move his touch where she needed it.

He pushed the fabric of her panties aside and lightly traced the opening of her body. She was so ready for him. It was only the fact that he wanted to bring her to climax at least once before he entered her body that enabled him to keep his own needs in check.

She shifted against him and he entered her body with just the tip of one finger. He teased them both with a few short thrusts.

"Marco…" she said, her voice breathless and airy.

"Yes, *mi' angela?*"

"I need more."

"Is this better?" he asked, pushing his finger deep inside of her.

"Yes," she said. Her hips rocked against his finger for a few strokes before she once again needed more.

"Marco, please."

He pulled his finger from her body and traced it around her pulsing center of her need. Her eyes widened and she moved frantically against him. She leaned forward, her breasts brushing against his cheek as she braced her hands on the back of the lounge chair.

He turned his head and drew one beaded nipple into his mouth, suckling her deeply as he plunged two fingers into her body. He kept his thumb on her center and worked his fingers until she threw her head back and called his name.

He felt her tighten around his fingers. She kept rocking against him for a few more seconds and then collapsed.

He tipped her head toward his so he could taste her mouth. He told himself to take it slowly, that Virginia wasn't used to him. But one taste of her lips and he was out of control.

He kissed her and held her at his mercy, caressing her back and spine, scraping his nails down the line of her back down the indentation above her buttocks.

She closed her eyes and held her breath as he returned his fingers to one nipple. It was velvety compared to the satin smoothness of her breast. He brushed his finger back and forth until she bit her lower lip and shifted on his lap.

She moaned, a sweet sound that nearly did him in. He reached between them and unzipped his pants, freeing his erection. She cried out softly as he brushed the tip against her humid center.

She reached between them and touched him, her small hand engulfing the length as she shifted to put the tip inside her body.

He held her still with a hand on the small of her

back. He had a lap full of woman, and he wanted Virginia more than he'd wanted any woman in a long time. Maintaining control was harder than it had ever been. Dangerous. He knew better than to let this mean anything more than a passionate encounter.

This was about the physical. One night together.

She rocked her hips, trying to take him deeper, and he knew the time for teasing was at an end.

"Marco?"

"Hmm?"

"Are you going to take me?" she asked.

"Do you want more?" he asked.

She leaned down and sucked his lower lip into her mouth, biting gently. "You know I do."

"Beg me to take you, *mi' angela bella.*"

"Take me, Marco. Make me yours."

He did want to make her his, in this moment with the night sky around them, the Southern Cross shining in the sky, he was away from Italy and the curse that had dogged the Moretti men for too long.

He was going to claim Virginia as his...even if only for this one night.

He gave her another inch, thrusting his hips up into her sweet, tight body. Her eyes were closed, her hips moving subtly against him, and when he blew on her nipples he saw gooseflesh spread down her body.

He loved the way she reacted to his mouth on her. He sucked on the skin at the base of her neck as he thrust all the way home, sheathing his entire length in her body. He knew he was leaving a mark with his mouth and that pleased him. He wanted her to remember this moment and what they had done when she was alone later.

He kept kissing and rubbing, pinching her nipples until her hands clenched in his hair and she rocked her hips harder against him. He lifted his hips, thrusting up against her.

"Come with me," he whispered to her in Italian.

She nodded and he realized she understood his native tongue. Her eyes widened with each inch he gave her. She clutched at his hips, holding him to her, eyes half-closed and her head tipped back.

He caught one of her nipples in his teeth, scraping very gently. She started to tighten around him. Her hips moving faster, demanding more, but he kept the pace slow, steady, building the pleasure between them.

He varied his thrusts, finding a rhythm that would draw out the tension at the base of his spine. Something that would make his time in her body, wrapped in her silky limbs, seem to last forever.

"Hold on to me tightly."

She did as he asked and he rolled them over so that she was beneath him. He pushed her legs up against her body so that he could thrust deeper, so that she was open and vulnerable to him.

"Now, Virginia," he said.

She nodded and he felt her body tighten. Then she

scraped her nails down his back, clutching his buttocks and drawing him in. Blood roared in his ears as he felt everything in his world center on this one woman.

He called her name as he came. He saw her eyes widen and felt the minute contractions of her body around his as she was consumed by her orgasm.

He rotated his hips against her until she stopped rocking against him. She wrapped her arms around his shoulders and kissed the underside of his chin.

"Oh, Marco," she said. "Thank you for making love to me."

"You're very welcome, Virginia."

She wrapped her arms around him and held him close. "I never thought it would be like this."

"Like what?"

"So incredible. Being with you is just…well, I had no idea it would be so raw and intense."

He laughed. "That's because you hadn't made love with me before."

She tipped her head back and in her eyes he saw a vulnerability that he didn't understand.

"I think you are right."

Marco stretched and rolled over as the morning sunlight spread across the floor of his bedroom. The pillow next to his was rumpled and the sheets still smelled faintly of sex and Virginia's perfume.

"Cara mia?"

There was no answer as he stood up and stretched.

There was a glass of juice on his nightstand. He smiled as he reached for it. Maybe Virginia was making breakfast for them.

He walked slowly through his penthouse. All of Melbourne was spread out before him, and he thought for a moment about his life and the fact that he seemed to have it all. He wondered about the curse of Nonno's that had doomed their family. He'd never put too much stock in it, preferring to believe that he had control over his own destiny, but Dom had loved and lost badly, so perhaps there *was* something to the Moretti curse.

He scrubbed a hand over his face. Why was he thinking about that damned curse this morning?

He didn't want to admit it was because he liked Virginia. He was tempted to postpone his travel plans today. Stay in Melbourne with her as long as he could before commitments would demand he leave.

And that was the true measure of why she really did need to leave. He'd find her, eat whatever it was she'd fixed for him and then send her on her way.

"Virginia?"

Still no answer. The kitchen was empty. Maybe she was on the balcony. He remembered that last night she'd really enjoyed being outside. He stopped in his office, noticing that the papers on his desk were askew, as if someone had riffled through them. Knowing how important it was to keep the Moretti Motors secrets, Marco started to grow concerned.

Had Virginia been in his penthouse just to find out what Moretti Motors was doing?

Hell, now he was getting paranoid like Dom. She hadn't asked a single question about the company and hadn't really seemed interested in it.

He finally got to the balcony and it was empty, as well. He realized she was gone. He knew it wasn't hard to leave. The keypad at the elevator only prevented people from entering.

Marco clenched his fists, angry that Virginia had left before he'd had a chance to…hell, he wasn't ready for her to leave yet. He'd thought about changing his entire day for her, and she was gone.

Four

The race in Barcelona, Spain, wasn't any different from the two previous races for Marco. He did press conferences, attended Moretti Motors functions and as far as his brothers and his teammate Keke were concerned, he was the same ambitious winning driver he'd always been.

But inside Marco seethed. At first, when he'd discovered he was alone in Melbourne, he'd been concerned about Virginia, worried that their night of passion had overwhelmed her. But as time had gone on he'd realized that she'd been after just that one night with him.

He also realized that she didn't want to be found. And that shouldn't have been a big deal. He was aware that if she'd stayed, he would have hustled her out of the penthouse and then gone on with his life. He wasn't looking to settle down. He had made a promise to his brothers that he wouldn't break, and he had no time in his life for romantic complications.

So why, then, was he still so angry when he thought about the way she'd left him?

"Marco?"

"*Sì?*"

"We have to meet with the officials in a few minutes…are you okay?" Keke asked.

"Fine. Just going through the race in my head."

"Are you free for dinner tonight? Elena's family is in town and we're going out with them."

Keke and Elena were getting more serious with each month that passed, and he appreciated his friend always including him, but Marco was starting to feel like a third wheel with them.

"My parents are coming to the race, so I'm going to spend the evening with them."

"You can invite them, as well."

"What's up? Don't you want to be alone with Elena's parents?"

Keke flushed. "It's not that. I'm going to ask her to marry me and I would like to have you there. I don't have any real family, you know?"

Marco understood. "I'd be honored to join you. In fact, Dom has reserved a restaurant for our evening so that we would have privacy…would you like to use that location?"

"I made reservations at Stella Luna," Keke said.

"Then we will join you there. What time?"

"Nine."

Marco looked at the German, wondering what this would mean for their friendship. He knew no matter how much a man wanted his relationships to remain intact, once a man got married, his life changed. "Congratulations, *amico mio*."

"Thanks. I…if she says yes, will you be my best man?"

"She will say yes, and I will be your best man."

Keke left a few minutes later and Marco called his parents and brothers to invite them to join Keke's dinner celebration.

Marco had a moment's pause, as he always did when he thought of marriage. The plan that he and Dom and Tony had concocted when they were young boys meant that they'd probably never marry for love. And he envied his friend that relationship.

He left the garage and found a group of fans waiting for autographs. He stopped, smiled for photos and signed hats and shirts, all the while scanning the crowd for Virginia's face. He was a sap and an idiot to keep looking for her. She was gone. And he needed to move past that one night in Melbourne.

But he couldn't. She was the one who left. A part of him acknowledged that it was wounded pride that made him want to see her again. Another part, the baser part, wanted to see her again for purely sexual reasons. He wanted to take her and enslave her with the passion that ran between them. Bind her to him and then when she was well and truly his…leave her so that she could experience what he'd been going through.

He was lucky his racing hadn't suffered, but at this point in his career he knew how to shut out everything except the race when he got behind the wheel.

"Marco, wait up," Dom called as he walked across the field toward him.

"What is it?"

"I got your message about tonight and I'll try to be there. But I may not be available."

"Is something going on?"

"I think we have a spy in our company. I might have to return to Milan to take care of the matter."

Marco's eyes narrowed. *The ruffled papers on my desk….* "Why do you think that?"

"I ran into Dirk Buchard today in the owner's lounge, and he mentioned rumors of a new car design from ESP," Dom said.

ESP Motors had been formed by Nonno's archrival on the Grand Prix track. Moretti Motors had outshone ESP at the time. One thing that had been in Lorenzo's favor was the fact that he had the Midas touch when it came to business. "What about the design?"

"I might be paranoid—"

Marco snorted. His brother wrote the book on paranoid when it came to guarding business secrets. "*Might* be?"

"Whatever. But he mentioned something that is on the new Vallerio model. And no one outside of you, me, Antonio and our R & D team has seen that."

"You don't have to stay for the race if you want to go back to Milan and do some more research," Marco said.

"I want to. I think you race better when Tony and I are here."

"I agree. I like to remind you both that I'm faster than either of you can ever hope to be."

Dom punched him in the arm. "Speed isn't the only thing that matters."

"In our world it is."

"True enough. Speaking of speed, did you get the e-mail I sent about the new marketing campaign?"

"Yes. I like it. I think it'll be just what we need to launch the new Vallerio."

"I agree."

Marco thought for a moment. "Is it possible that someone could have figured out what we were doing by studying the cars? I'm using similar technology in my race car this season."

"I'll know more after I go back to the Milan office."

Marco looked at his brother and thought of how hard they'd all worked to distance themselves from the fiasco that had been Moretti Motors under his father's management. At times like this, Marco felt like no matter what they did, they were always going to be struggling.

The only times he didn't feel that way were when he was on the track…and when he'd slept with Virginia. That night, he'd realized he could find peace in a woman's arms.

Virginia landed in Barcelona on Saturday morning. Last week, when her period had started, she'd had a genuine excuse to return to Marco. Clearly their one night of passion hadn't born fruit. She had been happy, because she'd missed Marco. And she knew that was a problem. What if her actions just perpetuated the curse on both families?

The truth was, she didn't care. Every night she'd been away from Marco, she'd dreamed of him, rich and vivid images of the two of them together.

And not just making love.

She'd had strong visions of her and Marco with children dancing around them.

She collected her luggage and found the car she'd hired to take her to the hotel. She wished her grandmother was still alive so she could ask her about the curse she'd put on Lorenzo.

But she had no one. There had been a bit of sadness laced in the knowledge that she wasn't pregnant. For the first time, understood why her mother had been so happy to have her. A child meant the end to the loneliness that seemed to haunt each generation of Festa women.

She meant to end that loneliness.

"Welcome to Barcelona," the liveried doorman at the Duquesa de Cardona Hotel said.

She'd chosen a luxury boutique hotel in the heart of Barcelona's Gothic district. She smiled at the doorman as she exited the cab and walked into the hotel. It was odd to be traveling so much, yet at the same time, she felt like she was finally alive.

All those solitary years of staying at home on Long Island, going to school as a child and young woman and then teaching—it had been a life of nothing but routines; and now she had a mission. Something to fill her days. She felt alive for the very first time.

She had no idea how to contact Marco and knew she'd have to spend the day by herself until the race tomorrow. She wasn't even sure if she'd be able to get close enough to see him and had no idea what she'd say to him when she did get there.

She checked into her room and changed her clothes. She thought about hanging out in her room, but she didn't like the thought of waiting around for Sunday.

She knew that changing her life this year was about more than breaking the curse. She needed to find a way to be the woman she'd always dreamed of being. If she was going to be a mother, she didn't want to be like her own mother had been, that solitary figure who rarely smiled and never left their small house. She needed to get out and experience life.

She went to the F1 track and watched the practice

session, making sure to stay out of Marco's sight, but getting as close as she could to him.

He looked thinner than he had been in Melbourne, but he smiled for his fans and signed autographs. She started to approach, but there was no way to get through the throng of people. And then Marco waved to the crowd and turned away.

She watched him until he disappeared into the garage area, and then she left the track. In her year of figuring out how to get close to Marco, she'd gone online to the F1 message boards and made friends with a lot of people. Using those contacts, she'd been able to get into the exclusive parties after the racing events. Even the VIP areas.

She took a cab to the Picasso Museum, because the thought of going back to her hotel room was unbearable. She strolled through the museum and lingered in front of a Picasso painting titled *The Embrace,* which the artist had completed in 1900. It struck Virginia how little couples had changed over time. Nothing was more soothing than standing together wrapped in each other's arms.

"It's beautiful, isn't it?"

She glanced at the woman who'd spoken. She was tall and slender and very beautiful.

"Very."

"I love Picasso's work, before he started doing the abstract stuff."

"Me, too. He reminds me a little of Pissaro in some of his early work."

"I'm not that familiar with Pissaro. Just Picasso. Are you in town for the race?"

"Yes. How did you know?"

"I saw you at the party in Melbourne. My boyfriend is Keke Heckler."

"He's on the same team as Marco Moretti." Virginia didn't know if Marco had mentioned her after their night together. She realized that she hoped he hadn't. She didn't really want anyone to know about what had happened between them, especially since she had no idea how he'd felt the next morning.

She'd left while he was sleeping, afraid that if she stayed there in his arms, she'd forget her plans and resolve and just stay with Marco until he tired of her. Leaving like that was something that she suspected her own mother had done with Virginia's father.

"Yes, he is. We didn't meet at the party, but I saw you dancing with Marco. I'm Elena Hamilton."

"I'm Virginia," she said.

"I have a confession," Elena said. "I followed you here because I was curious about you."

Virginia tensed. "Why?"

"Because Marco has been asking about you. Questioning everyone, to see if they know your last name or where you went. Keke said he's never seen Marco so angry when he thinks no one is looking."

"I don't know what to say."

"Marco's like a brother to Keke. And I've come to know Marco, as well. He means a lot to me, and I don't want to see him being used."

Virginia was glad to hear that. Glad that Marco had good friends who looked out for him. "I'm not using him."

Elena glared at her. "I don't believe you. Just know that I'm watching you."

Virginia nodded as the other woman walked away. It might be harder than she'd thought to have a second night with Marco.

Marco finished the Catalonia Grand Prix in second place, but he didn't mind not winning this week. Keke had been unstoppable on the track. His friend and teammate had a string of good luck going that stemmed in part from his recent engagement to Elena.

Marco smiled along with everyone else. Dominic was happy, because a win for the Moretti team kept them ahead of Ferrari and Audi, which was really all Dom cared about.

Marco rubbed the back of his neck, realizing he wasn't as joy-filled as he should be. He needed to get away from Keke and the rest of the crowd.

He started to leave when he saw the familiar brown hair that he'd been searching for at each race since Melbourne. *Virginia.*

She was here. And he was going to get some damned answers about where she'd been and who she really was.

Fans swarmed around him as he made his way over to her. He didn't have time for smiles or photos, but he made himself take the time. His popularity was one of the things that was important to the success of Moretti Motors. He signaled Carlos, his security guard.

"Keep that woman here," he said, pointing to Virginia.

"Yes, sir," Carlos said, and went to Virginia's side. She arched one eyebrow at him and he guessed that she didn't like that he was keeping her from leaving. Too bad.

He took his time flirting with the women fans who were always waiting for him. They liked to pose with him and have their pictures taken. Today while Virginia was waiting, he said no to no one.

Why was she back? he wondered as the last of the fans moved away. He signaled to Carlos to bring Virginia to him. She didn't look pleased, but he didn't care. He wasn't going to give her any further ground. He was in charge, and it was about time she figured that out.

She slowly walked toward him, hips swaying with each step, drawing his eyes to her body. He was intimately familiar with her curves and longed to touch her again. When she was within arm's reach, he took her wrist in his hand and pulled her to him.

She gasped as her body came into contact with his. He was hot and sweaty from the race and he was pumped with adrenaline and something else. Something he didn't want to define.

"Hello, Marco."

"*Bongiorno,* Virginia."

"You raced well today," she said.

She was nervous. And that pleased him. She *should* be leery of him. He'd never hurt her physically, but he was angry with her and he wanted her to know it.

He cupped her jaw gently and tilted her head back. "I want answers."

"I'll give them to you," she said. Her eyes were wet as he lowered his head, taking her mouth with his.

This was no gentle seduction. He meant to be masterful, to remind her that he wasn't a man to be toyed with. That his passion—and hers—belonged to him.

He forced her lips wide and thrust his tongue deep into her mouth. She clung to his shoulders, her fingers gripping him tightly.

He heard a small sigh escape her and he softened his embrace—wrapped one arm around her and hugged her to him. God, he wouldn't have thought it possible, but he'd missed her.

"Come with me," he said. The track wasn't the place for this kind of reunion. She nodded, speechless, and he led her to the motor home he used as a dressing room and place to relax at the races.

He had a million questions to ask, but touching and caressing her made him want to take her. He needed to establish his dominance over her. She'd left him, and while it was true that one-night stands weren't out of the ordinary for him, he'd always been the one to leave.

"Why did you leave the way you did?"

She folded her arms. Her short, emerald-green designer dress brought out the creaminess of her skin. He tried not to notice.

"I…I didn't want to wait around for you to tell me to leave."

"Why do you believe I would have done that?"

"Marco, I know the type of man you are."

"What kind of man am I?" he asked, curious to know what she thought she knew about him.

"You have a reputation of living fast and large on the track and off. And I knew, just as I know now, that a simple girl from Long Island has little chance of slowing you down for long."

There was a certain amount of truth to that. But he suspected that wasn't the only reason she'd left. In fact, the more he thought about it, the more convinced he became that there was more to Virginia than met the eye.

"I have never hurried a woman out of my bed."

"It wasn't you."

She lowered her gaze to the side and walked around the living-room area of the luxury motor home. She paused to look at the picture of his family on the wall. From over her shoulder, he saw his family all posed in front of the main Moretti Motors plant in Milan.

"Then what made you leave?"

"It was me," she said, turning to face him. "I wasn't sure I'd be able to leave gracefully if you were awake and I had to walk away from you. So I skulked out while you were sleeping."

"Why are you back?"

She took a deep breath and walked over to him. She brushed her fingers over her bottom lip, which was swollen from his earlier kiss.

"I'm back because I missed you, Marco. And I couldn't stop thinking about you."

He didn't admit that he'd missed her, as well. "Good."

"Good?"

"Yes. I have to shower and change, then we will go for an early dinner."

He walked away from her before she could answer. She was here, and he was suddenly determined that she would never leave him again.

Five

Marco's attitude made it difficult for Virginia to do anything but follow him. He'd showered and changed in the motor home and then come out smelling wonderfully masculine, and she felt very much like a school girl enamored with a boy. Though there was nothing boyish about Marco. He was all man.

A man who was determined to set the rules of their…"relationship" didn't seem the right word to describe what was between them. But he was definitely letting her know that he was in charge.

Whereas in Melbourne he'd wooed her, this time he simply took charge. And as they drove through Barcelona, she admitted to herself that she secretly liked the forcefulness of Marco.

To lessen some of his impact on her, she gazed out the window. Barcelona was a beautiful city. Very Mediterranean in feel. Whenever she traveled outside of the United States…as if she was a world traveler, she thought. But both times, she had left her home country, she noticed how different the world was. She loved the architecture of the old buildings. She loved the streets lined with people walking from place to place. And she loved the way that Marco fit into this world. This was his place, and she felt very much the intruder tonight.

But then she'd always felt like an intruder, and being in beautiful Barcelona wasn't helping.

"What are you thinking?" he asked.

She didn't want to tell him what she was really thinking. She cast around her mind for something to say and remembered that Picasso painting in the museum where Elena had cornered her.

"About a painting I saw earlier at the Picasso museum."

"Which one?"

"*The Embrace.* Are you familiar with it?"

"I am. My mother is an art history teacher."

"Really? Did you grow up surrounded by art?"

He shrugged. "Not really. She tried to expose us, but we were more interested in cars and engines."

"All of your brothers?"

"Yes. And my father."

"How did your parents meet?" she asked. She'd heard via the grapevine that Giovanni and Philomena had a love match. That their love had meant the destruction of Moretti Motors.

"My mom was hired to buy art for the lobby of our building. My father took one look at her and forgot all about cars and racing."

"Was he a driver like you?"

"No. He did one twenty-four-hour race with his cousins when he was in his twenties, but didn't care for it."

"What's a twenty-four-hour race?"

"An endurance race that involves a team of at least three drivers."

"And you drive for twenty-four hours?"

"In shifts…usually each guy drives for three hours."

She couldn't imagine what would make someone want to do that. But then again, she was a little unsure of why Marco raced. Wanting to go fast, she understood. She even got that he wanted to beat other people on the track—but racing as a calling she didn't really get.

"Is it fun?"

He laughed a little. "No. It's more. It's exhilarating and a bit of a headache. There's nothing else like it."

"Do you drive through towns or around tracks?"

"Tracks, usually," he said. He drove through the streets of Barcelona with skill and competency, which really didn't surprise her.

"Have you done one?"

"Every year my brothers and I participate in at least one."

This was his world, she realized. She wondered if the child they had would be like Marco. Would he have the need for speed? And what would being raised so far away from the racing world do to the child?

For the first time, she realized that, while her plan was to fix this generation, she had no way of knowing what the fallout of her solution was going to be.

"I like the track at Le Mans. We've done charity events, too, where we compete against other car companies."

"How is that different from what you do each week? Is it friendlier?"

"Not really. But we do raise money for charity. One charity rule requires you to have a woman driver for one leg."

"Who do you guys use?"

"No one. We haven't participated in that one…my family is cursed."

"Cursed?" She wondered how much he'd tell her about the curse and whether she should pretend that she didn't know what he was talking about.

"It's an Italian thing," he said. "Our curse involves women."

"Being around women?" she asked, wondering how much he knew of the actual curse.

"No. But being involved with a woman. Okay,

here's the truth, Dom has always been afraid that either Tony or I will weaken and fall in love with a woman, and then our family curse will kick in. So that's why we've never participated in that particular race. I think he fears that if I met a woman who loved racing as much as I do, I'd fall for her."

Virginia didn't like the sound of that. That Marco wasn't going to fall in love. But that shouldn't matter to her, she wasn't after his heart, only his child. "You seem very successful, to be cursed."

He turned into a parking lot and pulled into a space, but made no move to turn off the car or get out. "It's not a curse like that."

"What kind is it?"

"As I said, it's one that involves women."

"From where I'm sitting, you seem to do okay with women."

"I do. But I never *fall* for a woman."

"So, do you want to fall in love?" she asked. She wondered if he was lonely like she was at times. It didn't matter how full his life was. Because of her grandmother, he could only be lucky in business or in love. Never both. And since he'd chosen business, that meant a lonely life.

"No," he said with a smile. "I'm still young and have my life ahead of me."

"Indeed. What about racing? Are you going to retire?"

"Not for another few years," he said, turning off the ignition and looking at her.

The smell of his aftershave and the leather of the seats overwhelmed her, and she was very aware of the fact that she'd made small talk to cover her nervousness about being alone with Marco again.

This was something she hadn't planned for. Being with Marco again wasn't going to be easy, because each time she was with him she didn't want to leave. But more than that, she realized that he wanted answers from her, and she was going to have to keep on her toes to stay one step ahead of him.

Marco led the way upstairs to his apartment. He hated staying in hotels, and since Moretti Motors always had a driver in F1, over the years the company had bought residences in all of the major cities where the races were held.

He was trying to be genial and laid-back, though he really wanted answers. But after that one passionate outburst he'd had back at the track, he knew he needed to rein himself in.

He didn't want Virginia to realize how much she'd gotten to him. And she had. Until he'd seen her again, he hadn't realized that he'd been searching for her in every crowd—that he'd been waiting for her at each race. And that each win and each loss was marked by the fact that she wasn't there.

He'd never let anyone have that kind of power over him. He didn't think he'd "let" Virginia. For some reason, she was the one woman who could make him react this way. Only finding out every detail of who she was would give him the peace he needed.

Dinner had yielded few answers. She was very clever at keeping the conversation off herself and on him. But he was determined to learn more about Virginia, and he wanted to do it without asking her flat out for the answers. She'd set the rules of their game by disappearing and by the very mystery of who she was.

"You're staring at me," she said.

"You're a beautiful woman. Surely I'm not the first man to stare at you."

She shook her head. "I'm not really beautiful."

"Beauty is in the eye of the beholder, and I find you captivating."

"Marco."

"Yes?"

"Please don't say things like that."

"Why not?"

"Because I'll be tempted to believe you, and you just said that you weren't interested in any woman for the long term."

"I did say that, didn't I?"

"Yes."

"But you're not really interested in the long term, either, are you, Virginia?"

"I don't know," she said.

He had no idea what she meant by that comment. Maybe she was just as confused about what was happening between them as he was. But she'd left after one night. Most women didn't do that.

He wasn't being a chauvinist or anything like that. His experience had shown him that women stuck around for a while. That only when they were convinced a man wasn't going to be the right one for them to spend their lives with did they move on.

"A woman who leaves while a man is sleeping surely isn't looking for 'happily ever after'…though I thought most American women were."

"Why would you ever think such a thing? American women are independent."

"My mother watches *Desperate Housewives.*" To be honest, he wasn't too sure about that show as a standard for American women. But Elena was American, and she wanted to be married.

"That's a TV show."

"Television shows are made popular by the way they exaggerate real life."

"Marco, that makes no sense."

"You are simply saying that because you don't agree with my theory."

"Okay, if you're right about TV echoing life, how do you feel about movies?"

"I think that, to a certain extent they reflect the view of what they are representing. You know, I'm not saying that movies and television programs are real life, simply that they mirror an attitude of the culture that produced them."

She was so bubbly with her passion for discussing this. He liked it because he could tell that she wasn't planning what she would say to him. She wasn't keeping this conversation all about him, the way she had during dinner. This was something real. An indication of the woman who was Virginia.

He still didn't know her last name, but he would before morning. He hoped to spend this night uncovering *all* of her secrets.

He would know everything about her body, of course—he was already intimately acquainted with the sounds she made when her body was suffused with pleasure. Now he wanted to know what made her mad. What made Virginia cry? What made her laugh and smile? He needed that knowledge and he would be ruthless about getting it.

"Did you see the movie *Talladega Nights?*" she asked him.

"Yes. It was quite funny, with that Will Ferrell."

"Um…by rights I should assume you are like the French driver in the movie."

It took him a moment to figure out that she was trying to say he might be gay. He saw the sparkle in her eyes. She was teasing him. He knew he shouldn't feel good about that fact, but he did.

He closed the distance between them, tired of not holding her in his arms. The last month had been too long. He'd focused on racing and on the promo events that went with the Formula One season, but every night he'd had passion-filled dreams of Virginia and he wanted to make them a reality.

"I think I've proven that I'm more interested in women than men," he said, drawing her into his arms. "But perhaps you need another demonstration?"

She put her hands on his face and rose up to kiss him with the gentle passion he associated only with Virgina.

"I have no doubts that you are interested in women. I was trying to make a point," she said.

"Instead, you proved that Americans think Frenchmen are gay. It matters not to me. I'm Italian, and interested in only one woman tonight."

"Me?"

"You," he said, sweeping her up in his arms and carrying her down the hallway and into the bedroom.

He put her on her feet next to the bed. As he stroked one finger down the side of her neck and traced the soft fabric neckline of her dress, shivers spread down her body. His fingers were warm against her skin and she wasn't really listening to what he was saying.

She simply watched his lips to see if he was going to kiss her. That was what she really wanted and needed. She had missed him. And though she'd had other relationships before Marco that one night in his arms had far exceeded what she'd expected. He'd marked her indelibly and she'd been unable to forget his touch.

"I'm almost afraid to believe that you are really here."

"I am here," she said. Truly, she was afraid to believe that he'd taken her back into his arms so easily.

He leaned down, his lips brushing over hers. They were so soft, yet so commanding. And as he sucked her lower lip into his mouth and laved it with his tongue, she stopped thinking and just gave herself over to the feelings that were swamping her.

When she was standing naked in front of him, he traced the scar under her breast. "Do you realize that this is one of the only things I know about your past?"

She felt a frisson of fear at his words. He could never know about her past. His family and hers were enemies. Real life Capulet and Montague stuff.

"My past isn't important, Marco. Only what we have when we are together. Make love to me."

"Why?"

She felt more vulnerable now than she had just a second before. "I want to know that I'm really here in your arms."

He bent down to trace the scar with his tongue. His hands cupping the weight of both her breasts, one long forefinger stroking up and over her nipples. She shivered in his embrace, needing more of him. He made her react so quickly…he was like a flame she couldn't stay away from.

She tunneled her fingers through his thick black hair and held his head to her body. He murmured something in Italian against her skin. Then she felt his lips against her breast. His mouth moved over the skin, tongue licking and teeth lightly scraping until she was desperate for more of him. She needed more than just his mouth lightly touching her.

His hand on her other breast just kept stroking lightly, until she couldn't stand it a second longer. She pulled his head up to hers and kissed him deeply, sucking his lower lip into her mouth and biting him. She shifted in his arms until her breasts were pressed to his chest.

The cool fabric of his shirt shocked her naked skin. She hadn't realized he was still fully dressed and she was wearing nothing but her silky thong. The thought of being naked in his arms was very arousing.

He stood back up and lifted her onto the bed. Pulling his mouth from hers, he bent down to capture the tip of her breast. His hand still played at her other breast, arousing her, making her arch against him in need.

She reached between them and stroked his erection through the fabric of his pants, spreading her legs wider so that she was totally open to him. "I need you now."

He lifted his head. The tips of her breasts were damp from his mouth and very tight. He pressed his chest against them.

She reached up to unbutton his shirt. "Leave it. I need to be inside you now."

She nodded, and instead fumbled with his belt, finally getting it unfastened. Then she couldn't get the button at his waistband open. "Damn it."

He laughed softly and brushed her hands aside so that he could unfasten his own pants. She heard the swish of fabric and then felt the warmth of his erection against the center of her body. He rocked his hips against hers, rubbing the length of his arousal against her feminine core.

She needed him inside her. She reached between them and took him in her hand, positioning him for easy entry. But she could get no more than the tip inside her body.

He held his hips still, and no matter how she squirmed or moved, he wouldn't budge. Finally she looked up at him. "What are you waiting for?"

"I'm waiting for you to really want me."

"I do. I want you inside of me right now. I feel like it's been a lifetime since we were together, and I've missed you so much." The words wouldn't stop coming, and she knew she'd revealed too much, but she couldn't help herself. "Please, Marco," she said again. She ran her hands down his back, cupping his buttocks and trying to draw him closer to her.

He gave her barely an inch. "That's all you get."

His words were breathed right into her ear and almost made her climax. She shifted in his embrace, trying to take him deeper.

"Marco, please, I need more."

"No. You were a bad girl."

"When I left?"

"Yes," he said, pulling his hips back and thrusting into her again, still just an inch.

She wanted him madly. She needed to feel him deeper inside of her body instead of just at the threshold.

"Marco."

"Yes, Virginia?"

"I'm sorry I left."

"That's good, *cara mia,*" he said, giving her another inch.

She shivered around him and felt the first fingers of an orgasm dancing up her spine. She clutched at his buttocks and tried to draw him deeper.

"Marco…"

"I want your promise that you won't leave me again."

"I promise."

"You said that too quickly, Virginia. Do you mean it?"

"Yes, I mean it."

"If I give you all of me, then I'm going to expect you to stay in my bed until I ask you to leave."

She looked up into those obsidian eyes of his and knew he was serious. This was more to him than just a teasing game that lovers play. And she couldn't help but want to give him that promise. It might be hard to keep, but she'd try. "I will stay until you ask me to leave."

He stared into her eyes for a long moment before he thrust all the way into her body. She felt marked by his possession, that he'd changed her and she'd never be the same again.

She slid her hands down his back as he thrust deeper into her. Their eyes met. Staring deep into his eyes made her feel like their souls were meeting. She felt her body start to tighten around him, catching her by surprise. She climaxed before him. He gripped her hips, holding her down and thrusting before he came with a cry of her name.

She slid her hands up his back and kissed him deeply. "You are so much better than I dreamed you were."

His deep laughter washed over her and she felt like she'd found her place here. And that was very dangerous thinking, because if she belonged with Marco, then what was she going to do when she had to leave him again?

Six

Marco woke in the middle of the night and sat bolt upright in his bed. The voice of his grandfather echoed in his mind, saying something about being too late.

Marco scrubbed a hand over his face and reached for the light on the nightstand, flicking it on before he remembered he wasn't alone. *Virginia.*

She was really here. After they'd made love she'd fallen asleep in his arms. And he hadn't minded. Because the last thing he'd wanted to do was question her when he felt so vulnerable. Damned if this woman didn't make him feel…weak.

Well, out of control. Like he had the very first time he'd gotten behind the wheel of a Moretti F1 racing machine. Virginia lay curled on her side facing him, one of her hands reaching toward him, the other curled under her chin.

Asleep, he could study her without having to admit to anyone that he was obsessed with her. He knew that Dominic had been particularly glad when they'd met that morning in Melbourne and Virginia hadn't been with him.

Had his brother seen something in Virginia that had made him wary of the attraction she had for Marco? Or was it simply Dom's normal fear that a woman would distract him from the quest to take Moretti Motors to the top?

It wasn't like Marco was ever really alone. There were always beautiful women who were more than willing to hang on his arm and go back to his place for a night. What had been different with Virginia? Or had it been *his* reaction that had made Dom more watchful?

Marco didn't know if he and his brothers had made a wise decision when they'd vowed to avoid women who could make them feel. Marco couldn't speak for his brothers, but he was tired of the emotional wasteland that was his past relationships.

He let no one close to him. And at the end of the day, he was alone. Of course he had his brothers, and together the Morettis were strong—but there were times when he longed for the happiness his father had found with his mother.

The kind of happiness that stemmed from love.

He shook his head to clear it. He wasn't the kind of man who needed love. He needed a powerful engine under his control. He needed the thrill of pitting himself against the other top race car drivers in the world. But *love?* He didn't need that.

He pushed himself out of the bed and flicked off the light so he wouldn't disturb Virginia.

Why did she make him feel? He was thirty-six years old and he had a good life. Why was he suddenly asking questions and looking harder at the choices and decisions he'd made?

He walked to the wet bar and poured himself a Di Saronno. He tossed the drink back and walked around the darkened living room. The lights of Barcelona competed with the stars in the sky. He'd like to blame his restlessness on Virginia and the questions he still hadn't asked her, but he knew it was more than that.

He leaned against the French doors, staring out at the night sky over Barcelona. It was quiet now, and he had the feeling that he was alone in the world. His thoughts swirled and he realized that winning the Grand Prix World Championship this year wasn't going to be enough for him. Because once he had another championship under his belt, there would be nothing left for him in the world of Formula One racing.

He felt sometimes as if he didn't know who he was if he wasn't behind the wheel of a race car. Being the face of Moretti Motors was fine, but that wasn't much of a career. And to be honest with himself, he'd known he'd always been a little bit embarrassed by the way women flocked to him and photographers sought him out.

He walked back to the bar and refilled his glass again.

"Marco?"

He turned to see Virginia standing in the shadows of the hallway.

"*Sì?*"

"What are you doing?"

"I could not sleep. Did I disturb you?"

She walked toward him and he saw that she wore his shirt. He liked the way she looked in his clothes. When she was close enough, he reached out and pulled her closer, tucking her head under his chin and simply holding her.

"What are you thinking about? The race earlier?"

He was tempted to say yes. It would be easy to say that he was rerunning the race and trying to figure out when he'd lost, but his mind wasn't on Formula One or even Moretti Motors. It was on this woman.

"No. I'm not dwelling on the race."

"What then?" she asked, pulling back to look up at him.

"I was thinking that I don't know your last name or what you do for a living. Yet, you know what my mother's career is and a million other details of my life."

She flushed. "Is that important to you?"

"Yes," he said. "It is."

She hesitated. Then, "I'm Virginia Festa. I was born in Italy, but moved to America when I was a year old. My mother, Carmen Festa, was a schoolteacher."

"What about your father?"

"I never knew him. He died before I was born."

The name Festa sounded familiar to him. "Where in Italy were you born?"

"In Chivasso."

He stiffened. That was where Cassia had been from. The woman who'd cursed his grandfather and by default all of the Moretti men. He had no idea what the old witch's surname was, because his grandfather always just referred to her as that witch. But there was something about hearing the tale of Virginia's life that put him in mind of his own family's curse. He hadn't believed in the curse until Dom's doomed love affair. That had been the incident that had made both him and Antonio consider what their *nonno* had believed.

Lorenzeo had told the tale of a girl from his village whom he'd promised to love, a girl whose heart he'd broken. In return, that girl had cursed him.

"So it was just you and your mother?"

"No. My grandmother lived with us, as well."

"Just three women?"

"Yes. My grandmother had done something rash when she was a young girl, and I think her actions doomed us all."

Virginia didn't know if it was because they were standing in the dark or because of the comfort she drew from standing in Marco's arms, but she suddenly wanted to talk about her past. Talk about the path that had led her to his bed so that maybe, at some point in time, he'd understand what she'd done.

"What does this have to do with the secrecy you've kept?" he asked. He drew her over to the leather couch and sat down. She sat next to him, drawing strength from him.

Virginia realized that she was saying too much. That she should just retreat back to the bedroom or use sex to distract him and then disappear again in the morning.

Except the last month had given her too much time to think, and retreating to her lonely life wasn't what she wanted. She liked Marco. That was something she'd forgotten to factor into her calculations—the human emotions part of the curse-breaking. She'd always understood that her grandmother had been truly heartbroken when Lorenzo had refused to return to their village and marry her. But she hadn't realized that emotions might be the one key component to spell-casting that she hadn't accounted for. To be fair, she wasn't a witch and didn't regularly practice magic. Her entire training—if you could call it that—had simply been to study the practices to find a way to break the curse.

It was a basic thing, using emotions, and something she shouldn't have forgotten. But this spell, the only spell she'd ever tried…

"Virginia?"

"Hmm?"

"I asked you a question."

She smiled up at him. In the dark, his obsidian eyes were fathomless and she realized that she was falling in love with him. Was it only because she'd selected him to father her child?

"That's right, you did," she said.

"Are you okay?" he asked, the Italian accent making his words seem more carefully spoken.

"Yes, I am… Actually, no, I'm not. I guess because it's the middle of the night, I thought that telling you about the past would somehow make everything okay, but now I'm not sure."

"I'm not following," Marco said.

"You asked me whether the mysterious way I've acted about my life has anything to do with everything between us….well, it has nothing, and everything. I'm not sure how to say this," she said, losing her nerve. The middle of the night was a stupid time to make decisions. She knew that, but here she was anyway, about to tell Marco…

"*Mi' angela,* don't do anything you don't want to. I simply asked because…hell, I asked because I want answers. I'm tired of searching for your face at races and realizing that you aren't there—and that I don't know enough about you to find you."

"I guess that my second thoughts aren't fair to you."

"Second thoughts about what?"

"Telling you the truth."

"Have you been lying to me?"

"Not really lying, just omitting stuff. Actually, I wish you'd just figure it out so I wouldn't have to tell you."

"Figure *what* out?"

She took a deep breath as Marco shifted on the couch and moved away from her. She was on her own any way she sliced it, and she had to remember that only a child would change either of their lives.

"I'm the granddaughter of the woman who cursed your grandfather. Cassia Festa, my grandmother, was heartbroken when your grandfather, Lorenzo, refused to marry her."

He stood up, cursing as he paced away from her before returning to stand in front of her, hands on his hips.

"I know this story. So, out of spite she put a curse on my family—on the men—so that no Moretti man could have both happiness and fortune."

Virginia nodded. It was hard to explain Cassia's actions to someone who'd never known her. "She wasn't a happy woman."

"Yeah, like the Morettis have been happy…we lost our home, Virginia."

"I'm sorry. It wasn't like she prospered after doing such a thing to your family."

"Why are you here?" Marco demanded. "Did the women of your family think of another curse to heap on us? I have to warn you, Virginia, it's too late. My brothers and I have made up our minds that love isn't something we aspire to."

She shook her head. He was angry, and she acknowledged that he had a right to be. But that didn't mean she liked the way he was yelling at her. She took a few steps away from him then stopped. She knew Marco wasn't going to reach out and hurt her, and she had lied to him.

"I am not here to place another curse on you. The women of my family…well, there's just me. Cassia died a lonely, bitter woman, and my mother lost the only man she loved. And I…"

"What?"

"I have spent the last two years of my life studying the curse and trying to figure out why my grandmother never married and had only one child, a daughter—my mother. And why my mother's life followed the same pattern. And I realized something as I looked at my family and the curse my *nonna* put on you. She cursed you with an ancient spell. One that has a backlash to keep the balance."

"I'd like to say I care, but right now I'm too pissed off."

"I don't blame you. But you are hardly a man who hasn't had affairs before."

"True enough. But I've *never* left woman in the middle of the night."

"I'm sorry, but if you will just hear me out. There is a silver lining to this."

He shrugged again. "What did you mean by balance?"

"The balance of justice. The balance of everything in nature. The curse gave my grandmother what she desired, but it also required that she give up something to get her wish. And she craved Lorenzo's unhappiness. She needed him to feel the same heartbreak that she had felt…."

Marco went to the wet bar and poured himself two fingers of Scotch. "Cassia sought revenge because she was jilted. And she got it. My *nonno* was unhappy in love all the days of his life. His marriages failed, though he did get sons whom he worshipped. My own father couldn't make the business successful, but he had the love of my mother to make up for it."

"I had heard that about your family. I'm glad that you and your brothers grew up in a house filled with love."

"Are you?" he asked caustically.

"Yes. My own home was filled with bitterness. With that expectation that life wasn't anything but a series of disappointments."

"Indeed, it can be. Why don't you tell me why you are really here? Is it for money?"

"No, Marco, I don't want your money. I want your progeny."

Marco wasn't sure he could handle any more surprise announcements from Virginia.

"My prog— You want to bear my child?"

"Yes," she said.

Marco poured another glass of Scotch and tossed it back. His emotions were in turmoil. This night was turning into an all-out high-speed ride. It was something he'd only ever experienced with Virginia. With her, he never knew what to expect and couldn't plan beyond the road he could see in front of him.

Then he realized what she'd said. She wanted his baby, so did that mean…

"Did you lie to me when I asked if you were on the pill?"

She flushed and turned away.

That was all the answer he needed. "God, is there one thing you've said to me that is the truth?"

"It's not like that. I mean—well, it is like that, but I've been lying to make things right. Doesn't intention count for anything?"

"No. Hell, I don't know. Why me?"

"Um…well, it doesn't necessarily need to be you. Just a Moretti man."

"So, again I ask, why me?" he asked, becoming even more incensed. He was half-tempted to call his lawyers and find some reason to drag her into court.

"You were the easiest Moretti brother to get close to. And when I looked at you and your brothers, I just felt drawn to you."

He'd felt a spurt of jealousy when she'd said it didn't have to be him. That jealousy was assuaged a bit when she said she was drawn to him, but he didn't like the fact that to Virginia he was just a means to an end.

"Why do you want my baby, Virginia?" he asked, still trying to get his head around the fact that she'd lied about birth control. He came from a loving family. He was always very careful to make sure he didn't have any consequences from his affairs.

She twisted a long strand of her hair around a finger and walked a bit closer to him. She wore only his shirt and he realized how small and vulnerable she looked. With only the faint lights from the bedroom and balcony illuminating the room, she seemed ethereal.

But he didn't want to trust the vulnerability he saw in her. She'd lied to him.

"It's all tied to the curse."

"Tell me more about this."

"Well, I think that when my *nonna* cursed your *nonno* Lorenzo, she cursed herself. It was as if by denying Lorenzo true happiness, she eliminated it from her own life and from that of successive generations."

"Your mother wasn't happy?"

"She fell in love with my father and they were happy for about three months before he was drafted and sent to war. I was born, and three days later she received word that he had been killed. She was brokenhearted for the rest of her life."

"But you were born in Italy?"

"Yes. Just after my father left, Nonna's mother

fell ill and she and my mom went back to Nonna's village to help. When Mom discovered she was pregnant, they decided to stay for a while. After word came of my father's death, I think Nonna hoped some nice Italian man would fall for Mom and marry her, but nothing worked out. We moved back to the States when I was one."

"And your *nonna?*"

"She'd had an affair with someone in her village. I don't know who, but the scandal of her pregnancy caused her to leave the village and move to the United States, where my mother was born."

Marco was getting a pretty grim picture of Virginia's family life and he could see why she'd want to find a way to lift the curse. But that didn't explain why she wanted his child. And he was just realizing that every time he'd made love to her, he hadn't used a condom.

"How did you connect the tragic past of the women in your family with me?"

"It is the only thing that makes sense. I finally pieced it together when my mother died and left me my grandmother's journal. I learned a lot about the *strega* way and the curse my grandmother had put on your family. Until then, I had no idea she'd done that. I just figured we were unlucky in love."

"You, too?"

She looked up at him, and he realized he was getting closer to the truth. This was a very personal mission for Virginia. He rubbed the back of his neck.

He was mad at her for tricking him and lying to him, but he wanted to get past this.

"Yes, me, too. I didn't want to spend my entire life alone and unhappy the way my mother and my *nonna* did. So I started researching the *strega* way and curses. I knew the curse my *nonna* had used, because Mom had given me Nonna's journal.

"When I started reading the history of love curses, I realized that they had repercussions on the lives of whomever was placing the curse."

"How do you hope to break the curse?"

"By having your child. The merging of Moretti and Festa blood in a new generation will bring together what was torn apart and reverse the curse. But I don't think we can fall in love."

"I'm not going to fall in love with you," Marco said, not liking the way she assumed he'd fall for her. She'd done nothing but use him for sex and lie to him. The irony of her actions wasn't lost on him. He was well aware that for his entire adult life he'd treated women as his playthings. "And I'm not sure about you having my child."

She flinched and wrapped her arms around her waist. "I'm not asking you to fall in love with me."

"So you are really here to help me out?" he asked.

She bit her lower lip. "Well, you and your brothers and your children."

"What will happen to this baby you want to have?" he asked. He'd been the victim of a fraudulent paternity suit when he was twenty-one and had vowed to never allow himself to be used like that again.

"I will raise it. You wouldn't be responsible for the baby at all."

He rubbed the back of his neck. He didn't think he could turn his back on his own child. Family was the cornerstone of everything he did—even racing. "I'd want my child to know me."

"Then of course we can work something out," she said. "I wouldn't keep your child from you."

Marco put his empty glass on the counter of the bar and walked back to Virginia. He stopped when barely a foot separated them.

"Tell me the wording of the curse."

"I can let you read Nonna's journal if you like, but I don't think I should say the words aloud. They are very powerful."

"Fine. Get the journal for me, please."

Marco watched her leave. She came back a few minutes later with a worn, leather-bound book. She untied the ribbon around the middle and opened it. He saw his grandfather's name on the first page. In Italian, there was the undying love of a young woman. Cassia wrote about her hopes and dreams. He put his hand over Virginia's to keep her from turning the page.

Marco knew he had to get over his anger if he was going to figure out how to move forward from this.

"Do you want to see the curse?" Virginia asked.

"Yes." He lifted his hand.

PLAY THE
Lucky Key Game

and you can get

FREE BOOKS
and FREE GIFTS!

Do You Have the LUCKY KEY?

Scratch the gold areas with a coin. Then check below to see the books and gifts you can get!

YES!
I have scratched off the gold areas. Please send me the 2 FREE BOOKS and 2 FREE GIFTS, worth about $10, for which I qualify. I understand I am under no obligation to purchase any books, as explained on the back of this card.

326 SDL EXE2   **225 SDL EW6E**

FIRST NAME   LAST NAME

ADDRESS

APT.#   CITY

www.ReaderService.com

STATE/PROV.   ZIP/POSTAL CODE

🔑🔑🔑🔑 2 free books plus 2 free gifts   🔑🔑🔑🔑 1 free book

🔑🔑🔑🔑 2 free books   🔑🔑🔑🔑 Try Again!

If offer card is missing write to: Silhouette Reader Service, P.O. Box 1867, Buffalo NY 14240-1867 or order online at www.ReaderService.com

BUSINESS REPLY MAIL

FIRST-CLASS MAIL   PERMIT NO. 717   BUFFALO, NY

POSTAGE WILL BE PAID BY ADDRESSEE

**SILHOUETTE READER SERVICE
PO BOX 1867
BUFFALO NY 14240-9952**

NO POSTAGE
NECESSARY
IF MAILED
IN THE
UNITED STATES

She flipped the pages to about three-quarters of the way through the journal. There was the same handwriting, only it seemed angrier. The curling script of earlier had become shorter and more compact, the lines of ink slashing across the page.

My love for you was all-encompassing and never-ending, and with its death I call upon the universe to bring about the death of your heart and the hearts of succeeding generations.

As long as a Moretti roams this earth, he shall have happiness in either business or love but never both.

Do not disdain the powers of a small body. Moretti, you may be strong, but that will no longer help you. I am strong in my will and I demand retribution for the pain you have caused me.

"What makes you think having a child will break this curse?" he asked.

"The part that speaks of retribution. My grand-mother wanted to create a family with your grand-father, and since he denied her that and placed racing above her, she wanted to deny him love forever-more."

Marco looked at the words again. He noticed a different handwriting in the column. These words were in English and not in Italian. "Is this your handwriting?"

"Yes. I have spent a lot of time researching the words Nonna used, so I could figure out how to break the spell."

"Can't you just reverse it?"

"No. I can't. Nonna could have, but she's dead."

"Okay, let me make sure I have this right. You are here to get pregnant so you can break the Moretti curse?"

She nibbled on her lower lip and then nodded.

"What's in it for you?"

"It will keep me from ending up bitter and alone like my mother and grandmother did. And it will give me the chance at a future with a husband and more children."

He looked at Virginia, pictured her growing big and round with his child, and felt a primal rush. He wanted to plant his seed in this woman. Not just because it might break the curse on all the Moretti clan, but because on some primitive level he believed that Virginia was his.

He made a gut decision. "Okay. In the morning I will have a contract drawn up that details this arrangement. You will travel with me for this racing season until you are pregnant. Then you will live in a house I pay for until the child is born. I think I should like for you to continue to live there with the child and raise the child close by me. I will have free visitation of the child."

She put her hands on her hips. "You will not be making all the rules of this arrangement, Marco. I'm not going to just do what you tell me to."

He reached out and grabbed her wrists, drawing her into his arms. "I think you will, Virginia. Because without my 'rules' you will have nothing."

Seven

Marco knew this meeting wouldn't be easy. Dom had always had a thing about their family curse, and bringing it up wasn't going to go over well. But since he'd called everyone last night and asked them to meet this morning at his parents' townhouse in Milan, he had no choice but to follow through.

"Bon giorno," Marco said as he entered the sunroom.

His mother rose and gave him a kiss on the cheek and his father hugged him close. As much as Marco was an adult, he still liked the feeling of coming home.

"What was so urgent we had to meet so early in the morning?" Tony asked, sipping his morning espresso.

Marco took a seat across from his mom and next to Tony. He served himself some food, even though he didn't feel like eating.

"It involves the family curse," Marco started.

The silence was electric. Then Dom spoke. "What about it? You know this is a crucial year for us. Does this have anything to do with that woman you were with in Melbourne…Virginia something?"

"Yes, it does."

"I knew it." Dom said. "I had a bad feeling about her."

"Maybe you were picking up on the fact that she's Cassia Festa's granddaughter."

Dom's face reddened. "Don't mention that name in our house," he said.

"What does she want with you, *mi figlio?*" asked his father.

"She says she's figured out a way to break the curse that Cassia put on Nonno and the family."

His mother leaned across the table. "How? Lorenzo asked every witch he knew, and all of them said that without the exact wording, it was impossible."

Marco stood up. "Virginia claims that the way to break the curse is for her to have my child."

"What?" Dominic yelled, his voice booming across the room.

"Marco, that sounds crazy," his father said.

"I thought so, too, but…just listen to this. When Cassia put the curse on Lorenzo, she was angry at the death of her dream—husband, family and future. So she wanted to punish him in the same way. Make it so he could never have it all. But when she cursed him, she also cursed the Festa women. None have found happiness in love. Virginia has studied the wording of the curse and believes that if she bears a Moretti heir, the curse will be broken because Lorenzo's legacy will fall to a Festa."

"Who would raise your child?" his mother asked.

"I am having our attorney work on the details. I want to share the responsibility." He paused, considering whether or not to share the rest. "Virginia thinks one key to breaking the curse is that she and I can't fall in love."

"Is that a possibility?" Tony asked.

"No," Marco said, quickly denying the charge. He wasn't going to entertain the thought of Virginia meaning more to him than an affair.

Dom nodded. "So, what do you need from us?"

"I'd like the both of you to come to the offices with me this morning to talk to our attorney. I told Virginia we had to have a contract if this was going to work."

"I agree," Dom said. "We'll be there."

"What about your mother and I?" his father asked.

"I think you two should wait to meet her for now."

His mother nodded. "I agree. But we do want to meet this girl soon. After all, she'll be the mother of our first grandchild."

* * *

The thing about the Moretti family, Virginia realized the next morning as she sat in a corporate boardroom at a prestigious law firm, was that they were a
family. That Marco and his brothers all stuck
together as a group was abundantly clear to her, and
as she sat at the far end of the table by herself, she
felt very small and alone—and very wistful.

She never had the kind of bond that Marco had
with his brothers, and she wanted that. Not only for
herself, but for any child she might have.

"Virginia, do you agree to the terms?" Marco
asked.

She hadn't been paying attention and knew better
than to just say yes. "May I have a few minutes to
review everything?"

"Certainly," Marco said.

Dominic Moretti was an intimidating man, and he
looked like he wasn't pleased to give her a few more
minutes. In fact, his face had gotten tighter as she'd
explained what she wanted and Marco's attorney
had taken notes, then relayed the terms of the contract Marco was proposing back to her. Antonio,
Marco's middle brother, said very little at first, but
surprisingly, he'd been the one to add a few stipula-
tions in her favor.

Virginia didn't have the money to hire a good
attorney, and she certainly had no friends here in
Europe who could recommend a solicitor. But that
was neither here nor there. She knew what she

wanted, and this was nothing more than a formalization of everything she and Marco had talked about the night before. But hearing it in this sterile setting made her feel kind of cheap and unsure of herself.

Dominic, Antonio and their lawyer left the room, but Marco remained.

"Do you understand everything as it's laid out?"

"I think so. I just don't want to throw away all my rights without thinking this through."

"I'm not going to agree to anything less than what's been laid out."

"I know," she said. Part of what drew her to Marco as a man—aside from his being a Moretti—was the forceful and determined way he lived his life. He was a winner on and off the track, and she doubted that he'd settle for less than he wanted.

"So what's the hold up?" he asked.

"Nothing. If you must know, I wasn't focused enough to comprehend everything when the lawyer was talking, so I just want a chance to read over the contract."

Marco came close to her side of the table and leaned against it. He was dressed in a fine Italian suit and he looked so good that it was all she could do to pretend she wasn't entranced by him. She hoped she was successful and he didn't notice the way she stared at him as if she were fascinated by him.

"Go on then," he said. "Read over it."

But she couldn't. The scent of his cologne teased her with every breath she took, and she was hyperaware that he was standing close to her. All she wanted to do was move beyond the lawyers and the contract, to the next step—living with him until she was pregnant.

That wasn't something she'd ever dreamed she'd have, and she wanted to begin this phase of her life. Even though they'd have this contract between them, for the first time in her life she was going to have someone to share her days with.

Her mother had never really been a participant in Virginia's life. From the earliest memory, she'd known that her mother was simply existing until Virginia was old enough to survive on her own.

She pulled the papers closer to her and skimmed over them. They had been prepared in Italian, but there was a translation into English. It didn't matter to her what the papers outlined. She knew that if she didn't break the curse she was going to spend the rest of her life alone, and probably sad and bitter.

She took a deep breath and signed the papers. And then pushed them to the center of the table. She stood up. "Okay, that's done. Let's get out of here."

"Not so fast. You didn't even read the contract."

"I skimmed it, and as you said, it's not as if I have much choice. You have something I want. Something I'm willing to do anything to get. So in a way, I've already signed a contract. I want your child, Marco."

"Why is having my child so important to you?" he asked. "It sounds like it goes beyond breaking the curse."

"You won't understand," she said. A man who knew what a real family was, a man who had the support of his parents, brothers and friends, would never be able to comprehend what kind of lonely and isolated life she'd had. There was nothing she wouldn't trade to have someone special in her life. She wasn't willing to be the sad by-product of a long-ago curse, the way her mother had been.

"Try explaining it to me. I'm a very smart man."

She smiled up at him. "I know you are. It's one of the things that attracted me to you."

"Dominic and Antonio are smart, as well. So why *my* baby?"

"I don't care about your brothers. From the first moment I realized the way to break the curse, I knew that you were the one I wanted."

"So not just any Moretti would do?" he asked, stroking his finger down the side of her face.

She caught his hand and kissed his fingers. "Exactly. It was you or no one."

It was only at this moment that she realized the truth of her words and how important he was to her. And she made a promise to herself. She wasn't going to let herself fall for him, because Festa women and Moretti men weren't meant to be in love.

Lorenzo and Cassia had proven how disastrous that could be.

Marco was used to traveling and doing promotional events. He gave interviews to both broadcast and print media and was entirely at home in front of the public. He had always craved the spotlight and freely admitted that he liked the attention.

It wasn't that he was an egomaniac, it was simply that he liked all the fuss. And now, in Monte Carlo, it was even better, because when he left this press event he'd be going back to his villa where Virginia was waiting for him. It was as if he'd finally found what he'd been looking for, a surcease from the manic lifestyle he'd been living to try to prove to himself that he had a life.

"What's your hurry?" Keke asked as Marco tried to sneak out the back door of a party sponsored by Moretti Motors.

"I'm not in a hurry," Marco said.

"Yes, you are. It has been this way since you hooked up with Virginia in Spain. I'm engaged to Elena, and I'm not as desperate to get back to my woman as you are."

"I'm not desperate, Keke."

"I didn't mean that in a bad way. I think it's good that you have something other than Moretti Motors to fill your life."

"I've always had more than the company. I'm known the world over for my party lifestyle."

"I am, too—that's why I know how empty it is. There's a difference between filling time and actually having someone to spend it with. Someone who means something."

"Keke, when did you get to be a philosopher?"

"I know that I'm not a smart man, but having Elena in my life made me realize what I'd been missing."

"What does that have to do with me?" Marco asked.

"Seeing you with your Virginia reminds me of me and Elena." Keke shrugged. "I'm starting to think there's more to life than racing…like maybe it's time for me to retire and settle down."

Marco looked at his old friend. He and Keke had been teammates for the last five years. Keke was older than Marco, and maybe it was those four years age difference that had Keke talking like he was, but there was a sincerity in Keke's voice that made Marco hesitate.

"I'm not retiring, and Virginia is just a girl."

Keke raised both eyebrows at him. "Whatever you say, man."

Elena interrupted them before Marco could comment, and then he watched as his friends walked away from him. Was he desperate for Virginia's company? Was that why he hadn't sent her away immediately, as soon as she'd started going on about breaking the curse?

A part of him knew it was because he'd never fully believed in the curse. What he did believe was simpler. He wanted Virginia, and the contract gave him a safe reason to be with her. He didn't have to worry about marriage or expectations of love from Virginia. But her having his child was huge. Having

a legal agreement seemed to make things simpler—
unless he was just fooling himself.

He made his way to the waiting Moretti Motors
convertible that he'd left in the drivers' parking lot.
He liked the city of Monaco. He'd grown up coming
here every year to watch the races with his grandfather. The Grand Prix de Monaco was one of the most
famous.

Even the car he was driving had been his grandfather's. He'd always felt a special connection to
Nonno Lorenzo, one that his brothers hadn't shared.
Nonno had said it was because they both had a passion for speed. And Marco had to agree. But now,
staring down at his grandfather's car, he wondered
if there was more to him than racing. Was there more
to the man he'd become than what he was—the face
of Moretti Motors?

Did he really need there to be?

He ran his hand over the hood of the car, feeling
the power and the miles that the car had traversed.
There was a bond between man and car. It was
something that he'd never really talked about, but
this old car of Nonno's had always been like an ex-
tension of himself.

"Ciao, fratello," Dominic said as he came up
behind him.

"Ciao, Dom. What's up?"

"Antonio and I need to see you tonight. We
strongly suspect that we have a corporate spy."

Since Dom had been worried about a leak when

they'd spoken in Melbourne, Marco wasn't surprised by this news. "I'm seldom at the office, Dom. I doubt that I know the spy."

Dominic pushed his sunglasses up to the top of his head. "The leak could be anyone. And I want both you and Tony to go over the information that has been leaked to see if either of you have insight into how it is getting out. You know our F1 program better than anyone. And I hesitate to mention this, but…we hardly know Virginia, and she's been living with you."

Marco narrowed his eyes and thought about the freedom he'd given Virginia at all of his homes. Right now she was alone at their family villa on the outskirts of Monte Carlo. And while Marco himself didn't go to the corporate offices, Dominic's office faxed him a daily report to keep him apprised of the progress on the new Vallerio production car.

"Do you believe that Virginia is responsible for this? The first leak happened before we even met."

"We need to rule out the possibility of her involvement. Someone may have used her as pawn. What do you think?"

Marco had no real evidence, but his gut said that Virginia wasn't interested in anything other than his sperm. She'd been up front and honest about everything since the night she came clean. "I will ask her."

"Do you think that's best?"

"Yes. She will not lie to me."

"Be careful, Marco, I don't want to see you hurt."

"By a woman?"

"Her grandmother is the one who cursed our family," Dominic said.

Dominic had a point, but then his oldest brother often did. "*Arrivederci,* Dominic."

"We will have dinner tonight at nine at the villa. Will we see both you and Virginia?"

"Yes. And by then I'll know if she's the spy."

Marco got into the Moretti sports car that had been his grandfather's. He really hated to think how similar he and Lorenzo were in many things. He was determined that they wouldn't both let the distraction of a Festa woman ruin their lives.

Virginia sat down on a stone bench and breathed deeply. She loved the gardens at the Moretti family villa in Monte Carlo. It had been only two weeks since everything had come out—since she'd told Marco what she wanted from him. She spent a lot of time in the huge, fragrant garden courtyard in the center of the villa. Every room in the villa opened into the courtyard. The second-floor rooms had balconies, too, and she had enjoyed sitting on theirs in the quiet by herself while Marco went to the track to do his qualifying.

Since she wasn't a race fan, she didn't mind not being at the track, but she was starting to desperately need to be in Marco's company, and that wasn't good. She had to remember that this relationship was temporary, and that once she was pregnant it was going to be "*ciao,* baby."

"I thought I'd find you here," Marco said. He wrapped his arms around her from behind and pulled her close. He nuzzled his head next to hers and dropped a kiss on her neck. "What are you doing out here all alone?"

"Enjoying the garden. It's so pretty and peaceful."

"And that's what you need? Is my lifestyle too intense for you?" he asked.

She started to say no, she didn't mind it at all. But since there was no future between them and she needed to keep her emotional distance from Marco, she held her tongue. This wasn't really a relationship, no matter how much it might feel like one when his arms were wrapped around her.

"Yes, it is. I don't really like all the attention you get. It's tiring to have to keep smiling all the time."

Marco tipped her head back and kissed her. The beginning twinges of desire raced through her body. She turned in his arms and lifted hers around his shoulders.

His tongue thrust past the barrier of her teeth and tasted her deeply, and she realized that this was what she'd been waiting for.

How could she miss one man as much as she missed him when he was gone?

When he lifted his head a few minutes later, Marco said, "The attention will wan once the season is over."

At first she had no idea what he was talking about. She wanted to take his hand and lead him to the quiet corner of the garden where there was a marble bench and enough privacy to allow them to make love.

"What?"

He smiled down at her. "What are you thinking about?"

"Making love to you."

"Truly?"

"Yes," she said. All she'd thought about while he was gone, was that the physical was all she really had of Marco and all she could ever really claim of him. And with that thought had come the creeping idea that maybe, if she played her cards right, the desire between them could spark into something else. Something lasting. And then she wouldn't be alone anymore.

She ran her hands down the front of his chest, lightly scraping her fingers over the fine, Italian Merino summer wool sweater he wore. He caught her hand and drew it lower until it was over his zipper. She cupped his lengthening erection in her hand and rose, going on tiptoe to kiss first his jaw and then his earlobe.

"We have a dinner date," Marco said.

"With whom?"

"My brothers," he said, drawing her hand away from his body. "We need to talk, Virginia."

"Now?" she asked, not ready for a serious conversation.

"Unfortunately, yes, we need to talk now. Then we can get back to you seducing me."

She flushed and smiled at him. "What do we need to talk about?"

He led her into the formal living room. "Can I get you a drink?"

She raised both eyebrows at him. "Am I going to need one?"

He shrugged in that European way of his. She was coming to know that Marco gave away very little of himself. And that made her feel always at a disadvantage. "I'll just have Pellegrino with a twist of lime."

"Have a seat, I'll get our drinks."

She sat down and then realized that she was being a little too biddable. But she really had no choice. She hadn't had a choice for most of her life, and all of sudden that seemed to boil up inside of her. How long was she going to let the actions of others dictate her life?

She stood up, ready to take action. "What is this about, Marco?"

He turned with both of their drinks in his hands. "Sit down and we'll talk."

"I feel like you're calling me on the carpet," she said. He reached her side and handed her the sparkling water.

She took a sip and tried to marshal her thoughts. But Marco was close to her, and the only thing she wanted was to have peace between them. For the attraction between them to continue to grow....

Oh, no! she thought. She *was* falling in love with

Marco Moretti. And to him she was nothing more than a summer mistress. A woman who'd signed a contract to have sex with him until she was pregnant.

"Virginia—stop it."

"Stop what?"

"Whatever it is you're thinking."

"I just want to know what is going on. Why do you need to talk to me?"

"There has been a leak at Moretti Motors. Proprietary information has shown up in our competitor's offices, and we need to find out how."

She was surprised by the topic. His company had nothing to do with her. "What does this have to do with me?"

"The information started showing up approximately three weeks ago," Marco said, tipping back his Scotch and draining it in one long gulp.

"Again I say, what does this have—" She put her drinking glass on the table as she connected the dots. "You think *I'm* the spy?"

"Are you?"

Eight

Marco watched Virginia for some kind of reaction. At first she seemed to cave in on herself, and then he saw anger. But anger didn't necessarily mean innocence. Yet in this case, he had the feeling that Virginia *was* innocent.

For one thing, she'd shown very little interest in Moretti Motors, although that could have been her plan.

"Are you going to answer me?" he asked, walking to the wet bar to pour himself another two fingers of Scotch.

"Do I really have to? I mean, are you serious that you think I'm giving information to another company?"

"I am serious," he said, turning back to face her. He'd never really trusted any woman. Maybe that was why his relationships were all short-term. He'd always put it down to the time he spent on the track.

"I don't know anything about your business, and I don't really care about it. This obsession you Moretti men have with Moretti Motors is detrimental to your lives. I think that Nonna had a point when she cursed your *nonno*."

Marco had no idea where she was going with that line of thinking, though to be honest he wondered if there wasn't a hollowness in being so obsessed with the company. His parents had never cared that Moretti Motors wasn't the leader in automotive design under his father's tenure, and they were insanely happy together.

"So my family deserves to be cursed."

"That's not what I meant," she said.

"What did you mean?"

"Just that Moretti men seem to think the world revolves around their car company."

"Don't paint my brothers with the same brush as you paint me. You don't even know them."

"From things you've said, it's pretty clear that the company is all you guys think of. There is more to life than being the best automotive company in Italy."

"We are the best in the world."

She raised her hands and turned away from him. He thought about pushing this argument until she got fed up and walked away entirely. He didn't need the distraction that she presented. He didn't need this vulnerability he'd discovered in caring for her.

Damn. When had that happened? He hadn't meant for Virginia to mean any more to him than any woman in his entire adult life had meant. But somehow, she did.

That was why her answer to his question was so important to him. He wanted to be able to trust her.

"Just answer the question, Virginia. Did you pass anyone information on our new Vallerio production car?"

"What is that?"

"A new luxury production car that is the fastest in the world and also one of the most expensive. We are launching the car later this year…but you already know that, don't you?"

She crossed over to him and stopped less than a foot away, putting her hands on her hips. "No, I don't. I don't even know who your competitors are."

"Has anyone approached you and asked about the Vallerio car?"

"No. How would I pass information, anyway?"

"You'd take it from my home computer or from the faxes that I get from the head office and then copy it and take it to your contact."

"You've obviously given this a lot of thought. Why would I do this?" she asked.

"The information is worth a lot of money," Marco said. He wanted to make very sure that Virginia understood where he was coming from.

"I don't need money, Marco."

She was really ticked off and he didn't blame her. "I didn't miss it. But Americans are obsessed with money."

"The same way that Morettis are obsessed with Moretti Motors. That's a path to emptiness, Marco, and I for one am not interested in an empty life. Have you learned nothing about me in the weeks we've been living together?"

He reached out and snagged her wrist, drawing her into his arms. She squirmed, trying to push away. "I'm still mad at you."

"I know," he said. But seeing the passion and anger in her had turned him on. And now that he knew she wasn't a corporate spy, he wanted her again.

"I think you owe me an apology," she said.

He leaned down and pressed his lips to hers, seducing her with his mouth. He didn't let go of her, but he felt her soften against him.

"You hurt my feelings," she whispered when he lifted his head.

"I did?"

"Yes. I don't like that. I don't want you to have the power to hurt me, but you already do."

He held her closer. He'd never thought of Virginia as fragile. The way she'd come to him and strategized to have his child spoke of strength, and he didn't like the thought that he might be a vulnerability for her.

"I'm sorry," he said at last. "We've known each other only a short time, but I know you wouldn't lie to me about your involvement."

He kissed her again, trying to say with actions the things he had no words for. He couldn't—*wouldn't*—tell her that she had made him vulnerable. Vulnerable men made mistakes, because they had something to lose.

Marco was just realizing that he did have more to lose than just money for Moretti Motors, and he didn't like that. He had to figure out a way to insulate himself from the feelings Virginia evoked in him.

Virginia didn't want to stop being angry at Marco, but she did. Life was too short, and her time with Marco was limited, so she let her anger go. She knew that he'd asked because he didn't know her—four weeks was hardly enough time to build complete trust—but she'd hoped that they were working toward that. Regardless of what happened between them as a couple, she knew that once they had a child, they'd have to depend on and trust each other.

She twined her arms around his neck and held him close, resting her head against his shoulder. She wanted to pretend that falling for Marco wasn't going to adversely affect her, but it already had. She was changing in an attempt to please him, and letting go of her anger was just a little thing—one of the many that didn't really matter to her as much as time in his arms did.

"Mi scusi, il Signore Moretti," Vincent said from the doorway.

Virginia liked Marco's butler. The man traveled with Marco and made sure that Marco had everything he needed.

"Sì, Vincente?"

"Your parents are waiting for you in the study."

"Tell them we will be right there."

"Sì, signore."

Vincent left and Virginia felt a sense of reluctance to meet Marco's parents. They had to know that her grandmother was the reason for their family curse.

"I think I'll go freshen up first," Virginia said.

"You look fine. There's no need to do anything."

"Yes, there is."

He arched one eyebrow at her. "What reason?"

"I don't want to meet your parents unless I look my best."

He leaned over to kiss her and she let the caring that she felt for him surround her. She felt safe with Marco, which was silly, considering he had the power to ruin her life.

"You look wonderful. They aren't shallow people."

She suspected that. Marco couldn't be the man he was without having been raised by two extraordinary people.

"I just…"

"What?"

"Do they know that I'm Cassia's granddaughter?"

"Yes, they do. Why does that matter?"

Virginia pulled away from him. There was no way for him to really understand the bitterness her *nonna* had felt toward the Moretti family. It was impossible to think that the Morettis wouldn't feel the same way toward her. That they wouldn't resent the fact that her *nonna* had ruined any chance at complete happiness for them.

"What are you thinking?"

"Why?"

"Your eyes are suddenly very sad," Marco said, carefully running his finger over her eyebrows.

"I'm thinking that if my grandmother hadn't cursed Lorenzo, your family would be a lot happier and so would mine. I don't want to see your parents knowing that."

"My parents are the happiest couple I've ever met. They don't feel the burden of the curse."

"Are you sure?"

"I promise you. I think because my father followed his heart, he has no conflict. Not the way Nonno Lorenzo did."

That made an odd sort of sense to her, and she had a moment of clarity about the curse. *What if it isn't really a curse against happiness, but a curse that dealt with not really knowing what you wanted?* Cassia and Lorenzo had each wanted something different.

Cassia wanted Lorenzo and needed him to be happy with her love and living in their small village. Lorenzo needed Cassia to understand his love of cars and speed and his need to make a fortune before he could settle down with her.

With a bit of twenty-twenty hindsight, she realized that Lorenzo had loved cars and racing more than he ever could have loved Cassia.

She pulled away from Marco. Was she simply stepping into her grandmother's shoes? Letting herself fall in love with a man who would never fall in love with her?

"Come and meet them. I think you will see that they aren't at all unhappy with the way things have worked out."

"I wonder why not?" she asked. Her grandmother had been utterly miserable every day of her life. She'd kept a picture of Lorenzo in the kitchen and every morning Cassia would look at him and curse him. *Every day.*

Her earliest memories were of a certain disdain… okay, to be honest, it was a hatred of the Morettis. Only as she got older and could ask questions did she realize that hatred wasn't helping the Festa women.

"Because my father finds absolute joy in my mother. He likes cars, but as he said to me when I was eight, there is nothing in this world that can compete with my mother's smile."

"He really said that?"

"Yes, he did. Then he kissed her when she came

out to bring us some lemonade. To an eight-year-old boy, it was a bit on the gross side."

"What was gross about it?"

"Kissing," he said with a big grin. Then pulled her close and kissed her.

He whispered something in Italian that she couldn't translate, and although she didn't want to look at it too closely, it felt to her that Marco was starting to care for her, too. She knew that she could never be more than second in his life, behind his love of racing and speed, but at that moment she wondered if that hadn't been Cassia's mistake with Lorenzo—not realizing that she could still love him even if he loved something else more than her.

"Ciao, Mamma e Papa," Marco said as he entered the den. Virginia was still a bit reluctant to meet his parents, but she stood by his side.

His father was seated at the desk in front of the iMac computer and his mother was perched on the desk next to it. They were both staring at the screen.

"Ciao, figlio," his mother said. "Your papa is trying to show me the Moretti Motors Web site…have you seen it?"

"Not yet. What is the problem, Papa?" Marco asked as he walked into the room. *"Mamma e Papa,* this is Virginia Festa. Virginia, my parents—Gio and Phila."

"It's a pleasure to meet you both," Virginia said.

"We're pleased to meet you, too, Virginia," his mother replied. Phila gave Marco a hug and a kiss and ran her hand over his hair the way she always did. He hugged his mother close for a minute and then leaned over his father's shoulder to see what the problem was. To say that Gio Moretti wasn't too tech-savvy was a major understatement.

"*Ciao,* Virginia," Gio said. "This is on the company intranet, and I think I entered the proper password...."

"Let me see what you typed in," Marco said, working over his father's shoulder. His mother drew Virginia aside and they began to talk quietly.

He'd always been aware that his parents were special. They had that something that just always made him happy to be with them.

That didn't mean he hadn't gotten into his fair share of trouble as a teen, but he'd always been aware that his parents had a bedrock of love for him and his brothers.

Virginia's cell phone rang and she excused herself to answer it. Even though she was on sabbatical from her work as a college professor of anthropology, she had students sometimes call to ask for her expert opinion. He was impressed by her knowledge and the rapport she had with her colleagues and students.

"She's a nice girl, Marco. I didn't expect that."

"What did you expect, Mamma?"

"I don't know. I just wanted to make sure you were okay and that this girl wasn't taking advantage of you," Phila said.

Gio got up from the computer and wrapped an arm around Phila's shoulder. "Antonio told us about the spy and Dom's suspicions, so we thought it was time to meet this girl."

"So you came to Monte Carlo?"

"Well, that, and I promised your mother a week at sea on our yacht."

"Marco, we are concerned about you and your brothers." Phila said.

"Don't be. We are big boys."

"I know that. How is the curse-breaking going?"

"Mamma, are you asking about my love life?"

She blushed and smacked his arm. "No, I'm not. I really don't want to see you bring a child into this world without loving the mother."

He watched his father hug his mother. "Tell us more about Virginia. Why does she want to end the curse? Cassia certainly never wanted to."

"How do you know that?"

"Nonno went to her when he was in his fifties and tried to rebuild the trust that had been broken. But she refused."

Marco didn't know that Lorenzo had done that. "I don't know about Cassia, but Virginia said that the women in her family have been doomed to live solitary lives devoid of love. She thinks if she has my child, the Morettis and the Festas will be free."

His mother walked over to him. "Do you like her?"

"Mamma, of course I do. She's very smart and sexy."

"Good. Will you two stay together after the baby?"

"I don't think so, Mamma. Remember, she believes that we can't fall in love, or the curse won't be lifted."

"I don't like that," Gio said. "We want a chance to know this grandchild of ours."

"I will have joint custody of the child, so you two will be able to see the baby."

"How will that work? It's silly to have a child, knowing that you aren't going to stay with the mother," Phila said. "Have you thought this through, Marco?"

"*Sì*, Mamma. I have thought about it a lot. Having a child is the thing that will break the curse."

"Are you sure that Virginia isn't interested in the Moretti fortune?"

"No, Mrs. Moretti, I'm not interested in Marco's money," Virginia said as she came back into the room.

His parents turned to face her. "This just doesn't make a lot of sense to me," Phila said.

"Mrs. Moretti, if there were another way to break the curse, I'd do it. But this is the only thing there is."

Phila put her hands on her hips as she looked at Virginia. "How did you figure this out? When Marco told us about this plan, I thought it was crazy."

"Well…my grandmother and mother both lost their men before they could marry. Both of them were pregnant at the time their lovers died, and both of them never loved again."

"I'm sorry to hear of such heartbreakingly lonely lives," Gio said. "But how did you reach the conclusion that having Marco's baby will fix this?"

"I studied the Strega lore that Cassia used to curse Lorenzo. There is more to love curses than just making it so the lover of the one spurned doesn't fall in love again. It has a backlash on the lover placing the curse."

Virginia explained her reasoning to his parents. Her body seemed to vibrate with passion as she stated her belief.

"Until the curse in broken, Festa descendants will have no happiness in love. And I'm tired of being alone. The only way to fix this is for me to have a Moretti baby."

Nine

After Monte Carlo and spending time with all of Marco's family, Virginia felt like nothing could ever be that intense. Dinner with his brothers had been nice, and she saw how close the three of them were. It was obvious to her that Dom wanted to make sure she wasn't the corporate spy, but by the end of the evening she felt confident he knew that the only thing she was interested in was Marco and breaking the curse on their families.

Still, the Morettis didn't really seem to like her. They weren't rude or mean to her, it was just that… she guessed it was that they didn't trust her not to hurt Marco.

Which she thought was silly. Marco wasn't the

kind of man who'd let any woman hurt him. He was careful to make sure that she was only allowed to participate in his life in two areas—in bed, where he made love to her, and in public, in front of the camera, where he made it seem as if she were his newest plaything—which she guessed she was.

The trip to Canada had been pleasant. She'd enjoyed being in Montreal, and Marco had taken two days out of his schedule to visit her home on Long Island. They'd made love in her bed in the small bedroom of the house she'd grown up in, before heading back to France, where they were now. It was the end of June and they were in Magny-Cours for the Grand Prix de France.

They were south of Paris and she liked the area. The race fans were sophisticated and some of them were cordial to her. Others thought she was distracting Marco and made no bones about wanting her to leave him to racing.

They were staying in a chateau owned by a friend of Marco, Tristan Sabina. The chateau was like something out of a fairy tale and the Loire Valley was charming.

Yet Virginia couldn't relax. She'd been feeling a bit nauseous for the last few days, and this morning had thrown up after Marco left for the track to take his practice runs.

She suspected she might be pregnant. She'd asked Vincent to get a pregnancy test for her. She was both hopeful and frightened to learn the result.

She was falling more in love with Marco each day. It was the little things he did, things that she knew probably meant nothing to him. Little things such as finding a book of poems by Robert Frost, who she loved. Or sitting on the balcony late at night and talking about the constellations and the legends that surrounded them.

She'd ordered a book of Russian legends off the Internet for him, and it was supposed to be delivered today. She knew he'd enjoy it, and that gave her pleasure.

A part of her knew that what they had wasn't real. But this quiet time together was nice.

There was a knock on the door of the suite. She walked across the marble floor, loving the life she was living. She had to stop for a minute and remind herself that she wasn't dreaming. That she was really here in France.

She opened the door to find Vincent standing there. "*Ciao,* Vincent."

"*Ciao,* Miss Virginia. You have a guest waiting downstairs."

"Who is it?"

"Miss Elena."

Keke's fiancée. They hadn't spoken since Spain, when Elena had warned her to watch herself around Marco.

"I'll be right down to see her. Where is she?"

"I asked her to wait in the courtyard. I know you like to be outside."

"*Grazie,* Vincent."

Vincent left and Virginia took a quick minute to fix her hair and make sure she looked presentable. It was hard to feel confident in her looks when she was in the same room as the former *Sports Illustrated* model. But Virginia decided she wasn't going to let Elena's looks intimidate her.

She went downstairs and stepped out into the courtyard. It was a huge landscaped area complete with a hedge maze. She saw Elena sitting on a bench a few feet away. The other woman turned and smiled at her as she approached.

"Thank you for seeing me."

"You're welcome. Why are you here?"

"Two reasons."

Virginia was a little leery of hearing them. "And they are?"

"Well, first I want to apologize. I was worried about Marco and I shouldn't have followed you like I did when we were in Catalunya."

"That was okay. I think it's great that you care so deeply for Marco."

Elena smiled at her. "I don't have a lot of friends, because I'm a bit…well, Keke says I have a forceful personality, but others have called me a bitch, and I'm sure I came off that way to you."

She smiled at the other woman, thinking that Elena was actually a very nice woman who cared deeply for the people she called friends.

"You didn't. Please don't worry anymore about what was said in Spain."

"Good. The other reason I'm here is to see if you want to sit with me at the race this weekend."

"Um…I'm not sure I'll be attending."

"I think it bothers Marco that you aren't there. When Keke and I talked about it, I realized that you might not feel comfortable with the other wives and girlfriends because you don't know anyone…so I wanted to invite you to sit with me."

"I'd like that, but to be honest I can't stand it when Marco is racing. I keep worrying that he's going to lose control of the car and crash."

"I worry about the same thing with Keke, but these men of ours, they know what they are doing. They've both been driving fast all their lives. I have a feeling the only place they feel alive is behind the wheel."

Virginia kept up the small talk with Elena, but a part of her mind was on the fact that Elena had named her real fear. That Marco would never be able to love anything other than the speed he found on the racetrack.

Since he'd started living with Virginia, Marco had started a new ritual the night before race day. It involved dinner alone with her under the stars while they talked about whatever innocuous topic either of them came up with. Both of them avoided mention of their families and their pasts.

Tonight, when he came out to the courtyard where he was meeting Virginia, he saw that the table was set for four and not two. There was a wrapped package with his name on it and a note in Virginia's handwriting that told him she was waiting for him inside the maze.

This villa had been his grandparents'. And though he barely remembered his Nonna Moretti, he had happy memories of the time that he'd spent here as a boy. His brothers and he would spend endless hours at the Grand Prix track, and his parents—who never seemed interested in racing—would actually attend the races here, even though Nonno had long since stopped racing.

"Virginia, *mi' angela,* where are you?" he asked. The maze in this garden was familiar to him, and he knew there were many hidden benches and places to get lost. As a child, when his brothers were ganging up on him, he'd come out here and hide. He'd had his last conversation with his grandfather in this garden, on a bench in the center, near the fountain that was topped with a statue of Nonno Lorenzo's prized Moretti Vallerio open-wheel race car.

"Come and find me." Virginia's voice came from farther up the path. It was soft, and he heard a hint of laughter in the tone.

"Aren't we a little old for hide-and-seek?" he asked, but continued down the path toward the center of the maze.

"Are we?" she asked. Again her voice came from

farther up the trail, but this time it sounded as if it came from the left.

Usually, he didn't like to play games. His life wasn't the kind where he often had time for these kinds of amusements, but with Virginia he was finding he was a different man.

No longer the driven Formula One driver who was focused on speed and winning.

"I had hoped to make love to my woman, but if you prefer playing childish games…"

She giggled. And he smiled. From what he'd come to know of Virginia, she'd had too little happiness in her life. And as silly as he thought this game was, he didn't mind doing this for her.

Plus, he was intrigued. She'd gotten him a gift and he wanted to find her and learn what it was. He'd never received a gift from a lover when it wasn't a holiday or his birthday.

What had she gotten him? And why?

"Marco…" she called softly, and he realized she'd stopped moving.

"Yes?"

"You're supposed to say 'Polo.'"

"Why?"

"It's a hiding game that kids play in the pool."

He was certain he had narrowed down her location. But wasn't ready to end the game yet. "But it is also my name."

"I know. I was wondering if you'd played that game as a child," she said.

He smiled to himself, realizing that she'd forgotten the rules of her own game. Perhaps she'd even forgotten that she was hiding from him.

He stepped around a bougainvillea bush and onto the cobblestone path that led to a small alcove near the back of the walled garden and maze.

"No, I spent most of my time watching *Speed Racer* and building race cars in the garage with my brothers."

"Cars? Why am I not surprised?" she asked, but her voice had moved again.

"Were you distracting me, *mi' angela?*"

"*Sì!*"

There was a kind of joy in her voice that he hadn't experienced in his own life in so long. He realized suddenly that winning another Grand Prix championship wasn't going to bring him that joy. This was what was missing from his life. He wasn't lonely. How could he be with a family the size of his? But he had forgotten how much *fun* driving used to be. Back when winning a race meant something more than another notch on his place in history. And maybe winning the record-breaking championship would restore his joy for driving, but…what if it didn't?

For so long, he'd had all of his hopes on the fact that racing would always be in his blood, but he was finding that maybe that wasn't so.

He didn't say anything else—and pushed those

thoughts from his mind. They wouldn't serve him well tonight, or at tomorrow's race.

He stood quietly and listened, slowly sorting out the sounds of the fountains in the garden and the sounds of his own breath.

He heard the small scrapping of shoes against cobblestone and realized that Virginia was moving again.

He pivoted in the direction in which he thought he'd heard her, but the path was empty.

He started in that direction, when he felt the air change behind him and her arms come around him, her hands covering his eyes. He felt the brush of her breasts against his back as she rose onto her tiptoes and whispered in his ear. "Guess who?"

He reached up and caught her hands in his, drew them down to his mouth where he kissed them as he turned to face her. Staring down at her, he realized that the joy he'd been searching for was right here. A feeling he'd previously experienced only when pulling gs as he went through the turns on the racetrack swamped him, and he realized that he had fallen for this woman.

Virginia was in a good mood, having decided to just enjoy the time she had with Marco. But although he kissed her with all the passion he usually showed, there was something dark and brooding about him as she looked up into his eyes.

She realized then that life seldom went as planned. She *knew* that, she thought with disgust. *Hadn't she learned anything during her childhood?*

"Why are you hiding in the garden?"

"I wanted a chance to be alone with you before Keke and Elena arrived for dinner."

"You invited my friends for dinner?"

"Yes. Is that okay?"

"Sure, I'm just surprised. You haven't seemed too interested in any part of my racing life."

"I didn't want you to think I was just after you for the attention that follows you around," she said. "I saw a special on television once, about some women who hired photographers to follow them out when they went clubbing so that they'd look famous."

Marco rolled his eyes. "Was this in Europe?"

"No, the U.S. But still, people do like the attention."

"But you don't."

"No," she said, taking his hand and leading him around the corner in the path to where she'd set up an ice bucket with a bottle of champagne.

"What's this?"

"I really wanted this night to be memorable for both of us because, well…" How was she going to say that she was pregnant and there was no longer a need for them to stay together? She'd never had a problem finding the right words. Never had any problem saying what was on her mind, and she'd never cared what the consequences were, but to-night…she didn't want her time with Marco to end.

And she had set this up—as *what?* She started to feel very vulnerable and a bit stupid. He was going to see through the night she'd planned and realize that she wanted to stay with him.

What was wrong with her? Where was the clear-headed reasoning she'd always had when it came to anything in her love life?

"What are you trying to say?"

She shrugged and realized she didn't want to say anything about the baby just yet.

"Let's have something to drink." She knew that drinking alcohol wasn't recommended for pregnant women, so she planned to have just a sip of the champagne.

"Are we celebrating something?" he asked.

She wondered if he already suspected that she was pregnant. She'd been nauseous for the last ten days or so.

"I want to toast the qualifying time you posted today. I think you made a new track record."

"Yes, I did. But that is what they pay me for."

She arched one eyebrow at him. "Really."

"Well, that is what Antonio always says. That I'm paid to be the best so that the world will speak the name of Moretti the way they talk about Lamborghini or Andretti."

"I think your brother is making light of your accomplishments. They should be praising you for doing your job so well. And we will definitely toast your new record."

Marco drew her over to the champagne stand. He poured the drink into the glasses by the bucket for both of them and offered one to her. "To fulfilling our duty."

"Yes." She tapped her glass to his and took a small sip, letting the sparkling wine sit on her tongue until the bubbles dissolved. In this part of the world, the champagne was good. Even labels she hadn't heard of before were exquisite.

"I noticed a package with my name on it…."

She smiled at him. "I got you a little something. It's kind of a thank-you for the gift of these days we've spent together."

"I have enjoyed our time together, too. In fact," he said, drawing her over to the marble bench, "sit down, Virginia."

She loved the way he said her name, the emphasis he put on the different syllables and the way that his accent made her name sound exotic. It made her feel like she was something more than just plain old Virginia Festa.

She sat down and Marco settled onto the bench next to her. She set her champagne flute on the bench and turned to face him.

He took her hands in his, and she wondered if this was going to be it. The point where he acknowledged that they really had no reason left for staying together.

A knot formed in the pit of her stomach and she almost jumped up and walked away. No matter what he said to her, there was no happy way for the relationship to end for her. Breaking the curse had seemed simple and straightforward when she'd plotted it out. But the reality of Marco had changed everything. He had ripped away her safety net and left her vulnerable. Because as she looked up into his deep, chocolate eyes, she knew that she never wanted to leave him. She never wanted to be anywhere other than by his side.

In childhood, she'd believed that once the curse was lifted from her she'd find a good man, fall in love and live happily ever after. She knew now that wasn't the case. She was never going to meet another man like Marco. And she'd already given him her heart....

Why didn't falling in love make this right? She had truly believed that love made the impossible possible.

"Why do you look at me like that?"

"Like what?"

"Like I'm about to do something hurtful to you. I don't like it when you are sad, Virginia."

"I'm not sad," she said. And she wasn't. She was bittersweet, she thought. "What were you going to say?"

He rubbed the back of his neck. "Stay with me until the end of the race season. I know we said you would stay until there was a child, but regardless of any pregnancy I would like for you to continue traveling and living with me until October."

"I'd like that." She took a deep breath. "Um...I took a pregnancy test today, Marco."

He stilled. "Why didn't you tell me this right away?"

"I couldn't find the words," she said. "I am pregnant."

He smiled at her. "Excellent. Then that means we are on our way to breaking the curse."

"It also means we don't have a reason to stay together," she said.

"I want you to stay with me. We're friends now, aren't we?"

"Yes," she said. "Does this mean we won't be lovers still?"

He shook his head. "I don't want the life we've had to change. We can live together until the child is born, and then we will begin our agreed custody."

Virginia felt like she'd gotten a reprieve and that there was now a bit of hope for the future—for a real future with her and Marco and the tiny spark of life within her womb.

Ten

Marco won in France, came second in the British Grand Prix and then won again in Germany. They'd passed the halfway point in the racing season, and it was sweltering this first week in August. Now they were in Budapest, a city he'd always loved.

Virginia had confirmed that she was indeed expecting his child. He'd hired a physician to travel with them and monitor her, after they'd had a scare with spotting and feared she might lose the baby in Germany.

Now he was at the track garage, avoiding Keke and his brothers. It was odd. They all wanted to talk to him about the same thing—Virginia. But where

Keke thought that having a woman in his life and finding a connection with Virginia was the best thing that could happen to Marco, Dom and Antonio both thought he was putting their future in danger.

His brothers had cornered him last night and told him he was putting Moretti Motors in jeopardy by staying with Virginia and taking the risk of falling for her.

He was somewhere in between his brothers and his friend. He didn't like the new vulnerability he felt, now that Virginia was in his life. Asking her to stay with him for the rest of the season was an easy decision. He'd had mistresses before. But he'd expected his feelings for her to wan the way they had with other women.

Instead, his feelings were growing deeper. He missed her when she wasn't around. She rarely came to the track with him, and a part of him wondered why she wouldn't watch him race.

He acknowledged that he'd never really driven for anyone other than himself. Even though Antonio and Dominic told him repeatedly that it was his duty to drive and win, Marco did it for himself. He needed to be out on the track, beating everyone else and getting the adulation and the praise that came from winning.

He looked around the garage, realizing that this was one place in the world where no one expected anything of him. Winning was expected when he was on the track, but here in the garage, with his car nearby and the smell of tires and oil filling the air, he was just another driver.

"Marco Moretti?" a man called from the opening that led to pit row. The man was of average height, with thinning hair that he had unfortunately combed over his pate. He wore wrinkled khaki pants and a long-sleeved black T-shirt.

"*Sì?*" he asked.

"I'm Vincenzo Peregrina, with *Le Monde*, out of Paris. I'd like to talk to you for a few minutes."

Marco glanced around, looking for his crew chief, but everyone had left for the afternoon. If he hadn't been lingering in the hopes of avoiding his brothers, he wouldn't be cornered.

"I don't have the time right now, but you can contact Moretti Motors and make arrangements through my office," Marco said. He reached into his pocket and handed the other man his card.

"This isn't about Moretti Motors."

"Then what is it you wish to speak to me about?" he asked the other man. He didn't mind doing interviews and found the media to be very helpful most of the time. But this man wasn't part of the entourage that he usually dealt with.

"The young woman who is traveling with you."

"You're not with *Le Monde.*"

Vincenzo shrugged. "Would you have talked to me if I'd said I was with *Hello!* magazine?"

"Doubtful. As I'm not going to speak to you about this subject," Marco said. He saw Pedro, one of the security team who worked in the garage area, and signaled to him.

"Good day, Mr. Peregina."

Pedro reached for Vincenzo's arm, but the other man put his hands up. "I'm going. But you should know that just because you ignore my questions doesn't mean I'm not going to find out who she is."

"Your questions are of no concern to me," Marco said. He left the garage and went to the drivers' lot where his convertible waited. He climbed into the car and sat there for a few minutes. Maybe it was time to stop avoiding his brothers.

He didn't want the media to swarm around Virginia. He wanted to keep her private.

He dialed Dom's mobile. It was time to bring the full force of Moretti Motors into his personal life.

"This is Dominic."

"Dom, cio e Marco. I need to talk to you."

"I've got ten minutes before I have to go to a press conference about the new Vallerio."

"Did you find the leak?"

"No. But Antonio is putting together two sets of information, and we think we've narrowed the suspects down. We will see what information our enemy has, and then we should know who is our spy. Is that what you were calling for?"

"No, Dom. I just had a tabloid reporter ask me about Virginia, and I'd like to make sure that no one comes close to her. I do not think she is accustomed to talking to the paparazzi."

"That usually doesn't bother you."

"What do you mean?"

"Your women…you usually leave them to deal with the press on their own."

"Virginia is different."

Dom sighed. "That is what I was afraid of. We need to meet in person."

"Why?"

"Because you are forgetting about your blood vow to Antonio and me."

"What are you talking about?"

"You are allowing yourself to fall for her."

He uttered a curse under his breath, and his brother said nothing. Marco wasn't about to admit to Dom that it was too late, he'd already fallen for Virginia.

Virginia enjoyed dinner out with Marco. They went to an exclusive restaurant, and on the drive back he put down the top of his car. The Budapest skyline conjured up fairy-tale settings. The castle in the background and the warm evening air made her relax, and she forgot all the worries she'd been carrying around with her.

Marco had been treating her like she was fragile, and a part of her thought that he also saw her and the baby in her womb as something precious to him. Something that he wanted to protect and keep safe.

She turned her head against the leather seat and looked at his profile as he drove. He reached over and took one of her hands, brushing his lips against her palm before he placed her hand on his thigh.

He drove with the superb skill that she expected of him. And his concentration when he was on the road was intense. She was coming to realize that it was the same intensity he brought to everything he touched.

"What are you thinking about?" he asked.

"That you are a very protective man," she said.

He didn't respond, just glanced over at her.

"It makes me feel special to be with you like this."

He lifted her hand again, kissing her knuckles this time. "You are special to me."

"You are to me, as well, Marco. I never expected my quest to free my family from the curse to turn out this way."

He steered them through the streets back to their hotel. "What did you expect?"

"To be honest, I don't know. I haven't really dated all that much, so I don't have a lot of men to compare you to."

"And how do I fare compared to these few other men?" he asked.

She took a deep breath and the magic that was this night in Budapest filled her. "There is no comparison. You are so much more than I ever expected to find in any man."

"You make me sound—"

"Like what?" she asked, wondering if she'd revealed too much. But she had the feeling that he must have already guessed the depth of her love for him. She tried to keep her feelings to herself, but she was struggling with that.

"Like someone who's better than I really am. Please don't see me for anything more than what I am."

"What are you?"

"A Moretti. My loyalty is always going to be to my blood. My family comes first, and then racing."

"And I'm a distant third?" she asked.

She'd already known he didn't care about her in the same way she did for him. It had been obvious from the beginning that there was much more to Marco's love life than there had ever been to hers.

He was a worldly man, and that had never really bothered her until this moment.

"Not a distant third," he said. "I'm actually not sure where you fit. As the mother of my child, I think that makes you family."

She knew that Marco wasn't one of those men who felt comfortable discussing his feelings. He often told her how he felt about her body in very explicit terms when they made love. But he never spoke of his emotions.

He pulled the car to a stop in front of their hotel and she climbed out when the valet opened her door. Marco was already coming around the car, tossing his keys to the attendant.

"Excuse me, ma'am. May I have a word with you?"

Virginia glanced over at the man in wrinkled

khaki pants who was standing off to the side of the valet stand.

"No, you may not," Marco said. Wrapping an arm around her shoulders, he led her into the hotel and straight to the concierge desk.

"There is a reporter outside who is bothering us. He does not have permission to speak to us and I don't want anyone on your staff giving him information about where we are staying."

"Yes, sir, Mr. Moretti. I will take of the problem immediately. Perhaps you'd like to move to one of our other properties in Budapest."

"No, I would not. I have to race in the morning and I trust that your security staff will ensure my privacy."

"Of course we will."

Marco led them from the desk to the elevator. Once the car doors closed behind them, Virginia turned to him.

"What was that about?"

"That man is a reporter for a gossip magazine. He is digging around, trying to find out who you are."

"Thank you for making sure that I didn't talk to him. But I really don't have anything to hide. I mean, I don't mind answering a few questions, if that means he'll go away and leave you be."

Marco drew her closer to him. "*I* mind. I don't want him writing about you. I don't want the world to know the details of my personal life."

"If I didn't already love you, Marco, I would now," she said, and then realized what she'd done.

She put her hand over her mouth. "I mean…"

He pulled her into his arms and kissed her deeply, his mouth moving over hers with skill and passion. Bringing her body to life. Making her crave so much more than his mouth on hers.

"I'm very happy to hear that you love me."

Marco lifted his head when the doors opened on their floor. He kept one arm around Virginia as he led the way down the hallway to their room. Her confession made him feel ten feet tall. Somewhere deep inside he was relieved that she cared as deeply for him. But mostly, he just felt a primitive need to reaffirm the bonds between them. To ensure that she knew she was his and that no other man would ever have a place in her life like he did.

He wasn't sure if that meant he loved her or not, and he didn't care. Right now he needed to make love to her. To cement in both of their minds how deeply she was his.

He unlocked the door and led her through the suite to the balcony. He wanted to make love to her with the night around them and the beautiful city of Budapest spread out in front of them.

"Why are we out here?" she asked, her voice soft.

"I thought it only fitting that we celebrate out here under the night sky. Since the moon and the stars are what brought you to me."

"Did they?"

"Well, it may have been a *strega* curse, but the

strega get their strength from the moon and the night sky—"

"So they do."

She was so beautiful in the moonlight. It wasn't that she was classically beautiful, but there was something about Virginia that always drew his eyes to her. She imbued a certain sexiness that never failed to make him hard. Tonight, standing in the minimal light, with her hair hanging around her shoulders, she was breathtaking.

He ran his finger down the side of her face, caressing her cheekbones and her long neck. He reached the pulse at the base and felt it pounding heavily beneath his finger. "Are you excited?"

"Yes."

"Good," he said. He continued caressing her skin, tracing the seam where her flesh disappeared under the gauzy fabric of her dress.

She shivered with awareness and her nipples tightened against the bodice of her dress. He lowered the straps on her sundress so that the bodice hung loosely over her breasts.

"Take your top down for me," he said.

"Out here?"

"*Sì,*" he said. He stepped back and watched her. He wanted her to want this moment as much as he did. And he liked pushing her past her own sexual barriers. Slowly, she lifted one arm and then the other. She kept her breasts covered, one hand holding the fabric against her chest.

"Are you sure you want me to take this off?" she asked.

He nodded. "Do it now, *mi' angela.*"

Shaking her head and letting her hair fall around her shoulders, she let the bodice fall slowly away from her skin. Her breasts were full, her nipples tight, begging for his attention. She looked so sexy at that moment that he was almost overwhelmed, but he attributed it to the fact that he hadn't made love to her today.

He stepped to her and leaned down to lick each nipple until it tightened. Then he blew gently on the tips. She shivered, her hands coming up to frame his head. She arched her back and thrust her breast against his lips. He sucked her deep into his mouth and felt as though he could find that one thing he'd always been thirsting for in her body.

He wrapped his arms around her waist and drew her to his body. He attended her other nipple, and then tried to push her dress down her body, but it was too tight at the waist.

He found the zipper and lowered it. Her dress fell to her feet and he stepped back to look at her. She wore only a mint-green-colored thong and a pair of sexy heels. Her hair was tousled around her shoulders, her nipples red and beaded from his attention and her lips were swollen, begging for more of his kisses.

He caressed her body, sweeping his hands down her sides until he reached the satin fabric of her panties. He grasped either side and pushed them down her legs. Now she was completely naked.

"Now you are as nature intended for you to be," he said.

"Am I?" she asked.

"*Sì*. You are exquisite. And I cannot wait to thrust myself deep into your body and feel your silky limbs wrapped around me."

"You are a tad bit overdressed."

"Then undress me," he said.

She pushed his jacket off his arms, but instead of letting it fall on the floor, she took it to one of the patio chairs and draped it over the back. He enjoyed watching her naked body as she moved around the patio.

She unbuttoned his shirt next, taking her time to caress each bit of skin that she revealed. She lowered her head and dropped nibbling kisses on his chest. She pushed the shirt off and carried it over to the chair where she'd placed his jacket.

He realized that the minx was teasing him, and he was enjoying the hell out of it—and her. But he needed her. He wanted—no needed—to be buried inside her now. He was hard and he knew he would probably climax as soon as he thrust inside of her. But he wanted to make sure she came at least once before he did.

He lifted her up once she was back within arm's grasp and carried her back inside their suite. He set her on the couch in the living room.

"I need you. Now."

She nodded. "I need you, too, Marco. So much."

"Show me how much," he said.

She parted her legs and he saw the glistening of her body's moisture.

"Open yourself for me," he said.

Her thighs twitched and she drew her own hands down her body. But she hesitated at the top of her thighs. "I'm not sure I can...."

He took her hands in his and brought them to her mound. "I want to taste you, Virginia. Don't you want to feel my mouth on you?"

He kissed her lips again. Thrust his tongue deep inside her mouth and sucked on her lower lip before leaning back to see her reaction.

She nodded and he felt her hands move between them.

The pink of her flesh looked so delicate and soft with the red rose petals around it.

"Hold still," he said.

He leaned down, blowing lightly on her before tonguing that soft flesh. She lifted her hips toward his mouth.

He drew her flesh into his mouth, sucking carefully on her. He held on to her thighs, holding her in place as he carefully tasted her essence. He wanted to strip away all of her barriers, so that she'd never forget this night and the confession she'd made in the car.

He felt the frantic movements of her hips against

his mouth and then her fingernails dug into his shoulders. He lifted his head to look up at her.

Her eyes were closed, her head tipped back, her shoulders arched, throwing her breasts forward with their berry-hard tips, begging for more attention. Her entire body was a creamy delight.

He lowered his head again, hungry for more of her, feasting on her body the way a starving man would. He used his teeth, tongue and fingers to bring her to the brink of climax, but held her there, wanting to draw out the moment of completion until she was begging him for it.

Her hands grasped his head as she thrust her hips up toward him. But he pulled back so that she didn't get the contact she craved.

"Marco, *please.*"

He scraped his teeth over her clitoris and she screamed as her orgasm rocked through her body. He kept his mouth on her until her body stopped shuddering, and then slid up her.

"Your turn," she said, drawing him up next to her on the couch. She reached for his belt and he lowered his zipper while she unfastened it. He lowered his pants and boxers in one quick move. She took his erection in her hand and followed with her tongue, teasing him with quick licks and light touches.

He arched on the couch, thrusting up into her before he realized what he was doing. He pulled her from his body, wanting to be inside her when he came.

He pulled her up his body until she straddled him. Then, using his grip on her hips, he pulled her down while he slid into her.

He pulled her legs forward forcing them farther apart until she settled even closer to him. He slid deeper still into her. She arched her back, reaching up to entwine her arms around his shoulders. He thrust harder and felt every nerve in his body tensing. Reaching between their bodies, he touched her between her legs until he felt her body start to tighten around him.

He climaxed in a rush, continuing to thrust until his body was drained. He then collapsed against her.

"You are mine now, Virginia Festa."

"And you are mine, Marco Moretti."

"For now," he said.

Eleven

Virginia was happy to be back in Valencia for the Grand Prix of Europe. It felt like her life with Marco had started in Spain. She and Elena were in the pit area, hanging out together. The last three weeks since Budapest had been the best of her life.

She and Marco had turned a corner in their relationship, and contrary to ruining things, her confession had drawn them closer. Marco blew her a kiss from behind the wheel of his race car as he went out for a practice run on the track.

Elena slipped her arm through Virginia's. "I'm so happy for you and for Marco. He's needed a good woman in his life for a long time."

"Has he?" she asked. Though she knew it was silly, she was jealous of the women in Marco's past.

"Yes, he has. He and his brothers made that silly vow, and I thought that Marco would never date a woman like you."

"What vow?" she asked. She knew that no one, save for the Moretti brothers, knew about her contract with Marco.

"The one they took never to fall in love."

Virginia swallowed hard. She told herself that the vow Marco had made long ago had nothing to do with her. She was here to break the curse anyway, even if he had made a deal with his brothers.

There was a loud screeching sound of wheels on asphalt, and then a boom that shook the ground around them. Since her back was to the track, Virginia had no idea who had crashed. Elena's face went deathly pale as she stood next to Virginia. She gripped the other woman's hand as she turned toward the track.

Flames and smoke engulfed the car and she couldn't make out anything other than the sight of fire trucks rushing to the scene. Everyone went still. The only sounds were those coming from the emergency vehicles. No one spoke in the pit area until, finally, a man that Virginia didn't recognize came over to them.

"Keke isn't responding on the radio. They are cutting him out of the car now."

Elena started sobbing and Virginia saw her own

fears realized in Elena's eyes. "Is he alive?" Elena cried.

"Yes. I will take you to the hospital where he will be airlifted."

"Yes. That will be fine. But I can't leave here until Keke does."

"Do you want me to come with you?" Virginia asked. She wrapped her arm around the other woman. She had no idea what to say, how to offer comfort. Part of her was still afraid that Marco wasn't all right, though he hadn't been near Keke.

Her heart was racing. The acrid smell of smoke filled the air and the JumboTron screen rebroadcast the crash in slow motion. Virginia knew that if it were Marco's crash, she wouldn't be able to watch it, so she drew Elena away from the pit area and to Keke's trailer.

"How are you feeling?"

Elena said nothing, but silent tears ran down her face. Virginia hugged the other woman close. This was horrible. They knew nothing, and Virginia realized that the officials mustn't have heard anything yet. Elena needed someone to tell her something.

She saw a race official and waved him over. She used her rudimentary knowledge of French to try to communicate with him. "Have you had any word on Keke's status? His fiancée is beside herself."

"Nothing yet. Ms. Hamilton is welcome to go to the official trailer and wait there for word."

The official moved on.

"Do you want to do that?" she asked Elena.

"Yes. I think that would be good. Oh, God, Virginia, I'm so scared."

"Don't worry. Everything will be okay," Virginia said, then realized that she had no idea if everything was going to be okay. But she refused to think negatively. She offered a quick prayer that Keke would survive his crash.

"Let's go," she said to Elena.

When they got to the trailer, the officials were immediately very helpful in getting Elena a comfortable seat and a drink, but they had no information. After ten minutes, Elena turned to her.

"I can't take this. I just need to know that he's alive."

"Okay. I will go find out what I can. You wait here, so the officials can find you."

"Thanks."

Virginia raced back to the viewing area. She saw Dominic Moretti walking through the pit and ran over to him. If there was any man who could get answers for her, it was a Moretti.

"Dominic, do you know what's happening?"

"I'm not sure. How's Elena?"

"Beside herself. We can't get any information from anyone. I'm not even sure who to ask. But she needs something—to know Keke's status."

"I will see what I can find out."

"Grazie," she said, but didn't let go of his arm.

"Was there something else?"

"Um…have you heard from Marco?"

Dom grasped her shoulder in a very reassuring way. "He's fine. Still out on the track. They won't let him close to Keke's car, either. I'll tell him that Elena is anxious to hear from her man, in case he gets to talk to Keke."

"That would be great. Would you tell Marco… just that I'm glad he's okay."

"I will relay your message to him. Keep close to Elena. Here is my mobile number so we can keep in touch."

She programmed Dom's cell number into her phone so that she'd have it.

Keke was pulled from the wreckage of his car and airlifted to the local hospital. Marco had to finish his lap and still hadn't qualified. But knowing his best friend was in the hospital tinged everything.

Almost forty minutes after the crash, they were all back in the garage. Still wearing his jumpsuit and sitting on a chair drinking a bottle of water, Marco waited for the officials to reopen the track. Virginia had phoned to say that she was going to accompany Elena to the hospital. There had been fear and worry in her voice, and he hadn't had the words to soothe those fears.

He had no idea what was going to happen with Keke. He'd lost only one other friend to racing, but they all knew that it was a risk, driving at superfast speeds in cars designed more for speed than safety.

"Do you have a minute for us?" Dom asked as he and Antonio came into the garage area. His brothers looked tired and worried.

"Yes. What's up?"

"Are you okay?"

"Sure. Crashes happen. Remember the twenty-four hours at Le Mans, when we were kids? Everyone thought Nonno wouldn't walk away from that... but he did."

Dom and Antonio both looked at him and Marco knew they were two of the few people in the world he couldn't fool with his glib tongue.

"It really does not matter how many crashes we've seen. Keke is your best friend."

"I know, Dom. I keep seeing it replaying in my head. Keke—is better than he drove today."

Dom pulled a chair up next to him and sat down. "What do you mean? You think he deliberately crashed?"

"No. Not at all. He is too professional to do something like that. I think that he has something to lose now, and that made him second-guess his instincts."

Marco didn't say it out loud, but he was thinking that he had something to lose now, too. The new life that he was starting to carve with Virginia. He hadn't said anything to her, but he'd been thinking that once the racing season ended he'd go back to the States with her for a few weeks. Maybe convince her to move to Europe permanently.

"How do you know this? Did Keke say something

that made you think that Elena was a liability?" Antonio asked, as he leaned his hip against one of the big toolboxes in the area.

Marco shook his head. "Nothing like that, Dom. It's just that you get to know a man after spending so much time together."

"The same way that brothers know each other," Antonio said. "We look at the world the same way because we have a shared past and dreams of a successful future."

"Exactly," Marco said. He knew his brother was trying to allude to the fact that Marco had let Virginia grow too close.

"Let's discuss something else. Elena went to the hospital and will let us know once Keke is out of surgery."

"That is good. I'll head over there when you go out to take your qualifying laps," Dom said. "We need someone from Moretti there."

"Yes, we do. Is there any chance that the wreck could have been caused by sabotage?" Antonio asked.

Marco hadn't even thought of that. Had he used his perception of how Keke felt about Elena to color his version of what had happened on the track? "Why do you ask?"

"Because someone is out to ruin us. The corporate spying is one thing, but now that we are on to them, maybe they've changed tactics," Antonio said.

"It could be, but security here is very tight. Pedro would be the one to ask, but I have to warn you, he'll be offended that you are asking. He prides himself on being the best in the business."

"If he's the best then he won't mind a few questions," Dom said. "I'll talk to him."

"We need to be very careful for the rest of the season," Antonio said. "Marco, have you noticed anyone around here who shouldn't be?"

"Just a reporter who was sniffing around for information on Virginia."

"Are you sure he was a reporter?" Dom asked.

Marco rolled his eyes at his brother. "I'm not an idiot. Of course I'm sure he was a reporter."

"It never hurts to double-check. Speaking of which, we want to ask you something that is probably not any of our business."

Antonio, who always looked vaguely bored by the goings-on at the track, suddenly seemed very serious. They leaned forward in his chair.

"What is it?" he asked, alarmed by the way his brothers were acting.

"Do you remember the vow we took as boys?" Dom said.

"Yes, I do," Marco said. He thought of little else lately, with Virginia coming to mean more to him. He wondered if he was fooling himself when he thought that he could easily control his emotions toward her.

"Well, we are concerned," Antonio said. "I know that Virginia believes having your child will break the Moretti curse, but we're not so sure. And you are getting very serious about her."

"Since when does my love life concern either of you?"

"Since you are looking at her the way that Papa looks at Mamma. You know what that means as well as we do."

"She means nothing to me."

"Yeah, right. You are living with her beyond the original terms of the contract. You are warning paparazzi away from her and making sure that she's cosseted everywhere you travel."

"She's my mistress, Antonio. I think it's okay to treat her well."

Antonio and Dom both stood up. "Make sure that's all she is. We have all worked too hard to rebuild Moretti Motors to see it all fall apart because you fell for some skirt."

"I'm very aware of what Virginia means to me, and I'm not about to let either of you down," Marco said. He stood up and turned to go to his car, and saw Virginia standing in the shadows.

Virginia wasn't feeling her best after leaving the hospital and her wild taxi ride back to the track. She'd been out of sorts and not feeling too good already, and now her stomach was doing flips, because of worry, she suspected.

Seeing Marco had made her feel better, until she'd realized that he and his brothers were discussing her. And that he had just said she meant nothing to him. She was no different from the other women he'd been with in the past, according to what he'd just told his brothers.

She wanted to get angry, but she couldn't. She was still too happy to see him alive.

"I am sorry you had to walk in on this conversation," Dominic said. "How is Keke?"

"He's stable. Elena will be able to see him when he comes out of surgery. She's still at the hospital."

"*Grazie,* Virginia," Antonio said. "You are a good friend to Elena."

"I know it wasn't in the normal mistress arrangement for me to be nice to the fiancée of the second Moretti driver, but I figured I'd make the effort."

Antonio gave her a strained smile and said goodbye to his brothers before leaving. Dominic said nothing, and Marco had a tight, angry look on his face.

"Do you have a minute to talk?" she asked Marco.

"A few moments. Dom, will you leave us?"

"*Ciao,*" Dominic said as he left.

Marco turned and walked to his private trailer. A couple of his crew members were inside, but they left as soon as Marco entered with Virginia in tow.

He stopped in the middle of the trailer and turned to face her once they were alone. "I am sorry you had to hear that."

"I'm not. It's better for me to hear the truth. I had been fooling myself that even though you couldn't say the words, you still loved me."

"*Dio mio,* Virginia—"

"I know. You never said anything that would lead me to believe you cared for me. It was my own delusion. I think, once I realized the man you are…well, the man I thought you were…" She couldn't go on. She was going to start crying and that was the absolute last thing she wanted to do right now. "It doesn't matter," she said at last.

"Virginia, *mi' angela,* please don't let my words wound you. I meant nothing by them."

He came to her and tried to draw her into his arms, and she was tempted to go because he'd hurt her deeply and she wanted to be soothed by him. But at the same time she heard his voice in her mind. Heard him say that she was nothing more than a mistress, and she knew that if she had any chance of coming out of this relationship with her pride intact she needed to stand on her own.

She stepped back from him and he dropped his arms. "I do not know what to say," he told her.

"You didn't have that problem earlier when you were with your brothers," she said.

"That wasn't a conversation you were meant to hear," he said.

"I know. Believe me, you've done a great job of acting like you really care about me…but I guess that's what you usually do with your mistresses.

"I have no idea why this behavior surprises me. I knew that you were like this when I picked you as the Moretti brother I would seduce."

Marco put his hands on his hips. She saw the lines of stress on his face and also the flash of anger. "I'm not some kind of cad when it comes to women, Virginia. The women I am involved with—you included—have always come to me wanting something in exchange."

"How nice of you to point that out," she said sarcastically. She knew she should leave before she said something stupid, but she was too angry and too hurt to just walk away. She wanted Marco to feel the same pain she felt. That emotional pain that she honestly didn't know if she'd ever recover from.

"I'm not the one who slept with you and walked away," he said.

"No, you're not," she said quietly. "You also aren't the one who fell in love. Maybe this is the way it's supposed to be," she said. "I mean, I'll have a child and you'll have your life, which will continue on as usual. The curse probably demands that I shouldn't fall in love with you."

Marco remained quiet, and she knew she had to leave before she broke down and started crying. She had no idea that silence could hurt her this deeply.

"I guess I'll be on the next plane back to the States," she said.

"Virginia…I never meant for you to get hurt. I only wanted to keep you safe and happy."

"Well, you did a good job of that."

"Did I?"

"Yes."

"Then what has changed? Why are you leaving me?"

Virginia looked at him. He was a smart man, and she knew he had enjoyed the fact that she did love him. But there was no way she could continue to live with him when their versions of reality were so markedly different.

"I guess, now that I know how you see me…I can't keep telling myself that someday you're going to realize that the only way to truly break this curse is to fall in love and live your life in a fully realized manner."

Marco reached for her, and she felt his hand on her face. She knew this was the last time he'd touch her, and she leaned into that touch for a minute. "I'm sorry for making this goodbye so messy. And for not staying until the end of the season."

She kissed him on the lips and walked away while she still had the strength to do it.

Twelve

Marco didn't want to admit it to himself, but he thought he'd made a mistake when he let Virginia walk out on him. He'd won the Grand Prix championship, and in a few short months, Moretti Motors would release their new Vallerio model, if Tony had his way and successfully acquired the use of the name. His brother was already in negotiations to get that deal moving forward.

So Marco had no reason to feel like something was missing in his life—except that his arms felt so damned empty every night. He needed her back. Sometimes he thought he caught a wiff of her perfume in a room and would walk in expecting to see her, only to find that it was empty.

Empty.

God, how had he not realized that he was letting himself become the same man Nonno had been? He was letting racing and his public take precedence over his life.

He needed to do something, find a way to get Virginia back. But how?

He got his mobile out and called Keke.

"I need a favor," he said before Keke could ask why he was calling.

"What?"

"I'm going to get Virginia back and…"

"Are you coming to me for woman advice?" Keke asked, laughing.

"No, I'm coming to you because I need someone to help me coordinate things in the U.S."

"How can I help?" Keke asked.

Marco outlined his plan to his friend and a few hours later was on a commercial flight to the United States. Never before had he been so nervous. Not even when he got behind the wheel of his first F1 driving machine. And now he knew why. Racing was what he did, but Virginia was his life and his love, and he didn't know if he could survive without her. If this was how Cassia had felt for Lorenzo, Marco understood why she'd cursed him when he'd chosen racing over her.

He also thought maybe it was time for a Festa and a Moretti to fall in love and right the wrongs of the past.

* * *

Virginia spent the rest of the summer and the beginning of the fall in her quiet home on Long Island. She grew each day with her pregnancy, and the baby—a boy—was doing very well. She was still on sabbatical and enjoyed the quiet days at home.

She avoided newspapers and television and anything that might show her a glimpse of Marco. She'd learned the hard way that seeing him even on a magazine stand was enough to trigger a deep sadness inside her. A part of her wanted to say to hell with pride and return to him.

She really missed him.

But she also had to live with herself, and somehow she knew that loving a man who thought of her as nothing but a mistress wasn't a good thing.

It was a rainy Saturday in early November, and she was painting the nursery for the baby. She dreaded the thought of the upcoming holiday season—of spending another one all alone. But she rubbed her small pregnancy bump and realized that in a year's time she wouldn't be alone anymore.

She'd have her baby, and together the two of them would celebrate all the holidays. She was toying with naming the baby Lorenzo to appease the curse that Cassia had set. Maybe if she named her child for the man who'd originally been cursed, Fate would be happy with her and leave her be.

Her doorbell rang and she looked at her watch. That should be Elena. Her family lived in the Lake

George area of New York and she and Keke had spent the last few months there.

Keke had recovered nicely from all his injuries and had decided to retire from racing. He'd taken up a new gig, as a male model and commentator for a European sports channel.

Today they had both promised to come and help her with her room renovation. She had been grateful for their friendship. She'd never realized how alone she was in the same small town she'd grown up in. But she was grateful that Elena and she had become fast friends in the months they'd spent together on the Formula One racing circuit.

The doorbell rang again, and she realized she was dawdling. She didn't know if it was the pregnancy or what, but her mind tended to wander lately. Usually it wandered to Marco.

She opened the door. "Come on in."

"*Grazie,* Virginia."

It was Marco. Marco was standing on her front porch, wearing a pair of wool trousers and a black turtleneck, as well as a long trench coat. The rain had wet his jet-black hair.

"What are you doing here?"

"I hope you don't mind, but since you wouldn't return any of my calls, I persuaded Elena and Keke to let me come and help you today."

"That's…why?"

"Because we need to talk. May I come in?"

She stepped back and let him enter her house. As

he took off his coat and hung it on the coat rack she had by the front door, she realized how much she had missed him. He smelled just as good as she remembered and her arms were literally tingling with the need to wrap around him.

"You are staring at me," he said.

"I'm sorry. Why are you here?"

"Because I realized that I can't live without you. I don't care if my brothers believe that love is the one thing that will doom Moretti Motors. I need you in my life."

She wasn't sure she'd heard him correctly. "I don't—"

"Don't overthink this. I lied to you that day in Valencia, when I let you believe you were nothing more than a mistress to me. My life has been hollow and empty without you."

She couldn't say anything, but when he drew her into his arms she went to him, wrapped her arms around his lean waist and held on. "Marco, is this for real?"

"Sì, mi' angela, ti amo."

She tipped her head up to look at him, to see if the love he'd just spoken of was reflected in his eyes. And it was. She saw the sincerity there.

"I know I have no right to hope that you still feel the same way about me."

"I do still love you. It's been agony living without you," she said. "But I figured that was the only way to appease the Fates."

Marco shook his head. "The only way to appease the Fates is for us to be together. To raise our son and give him brothers and sisters."

"Are you sure?"

"Yes," he said. "Will you marry me, Virginia?"

"Yes!" She threw her arms around him and kissed him with all the passion and love she'd been storing up since they'd parted in August.

"What about your brothers?"

"I told them that we were all wealthy and that we would continue to focus on making our new production car very successful, and that was all we needed to do to break the curse."

"And they were okay with that?" she asked, not wanting his brothers to dislike her.

"Not really. But I told them that, regardless of whether you are with me or not, you own my heart and soul."

* * * * *

*The curse was lifted for Marco, but what does
Moretti's Legacy have in store for Antonio?
Find out next month in
Katherine Garbera's super-romantic,
super-sexy new story,
THE MORETTI SEDUCTION
On sale April 2009,
only from Silhouette Desire!*

*Celebrate 60 years of pure reading pleasure
with Harlequin®!
Silhouette® Romantic Suspense is celebrating
with the glamour-filled, adrenaline-charged series*
LOVE IN 60 SECONDS
*starting in April 2009.
Six stories that promise to bring
the glitz of Las Vegas, the danger of revenge,
the mystery of a missing diamond,
family scandals and
ripped-from-the-headlines intrigue.
Get your heart racing as love happens
in sixty seconds!*

Enjoy a sneak peek of
USA TODAY *bestselling author
Marie Ferrarella's*
THE HEIRESS'S 2-WEEK AFFAIR
*Available April 2009
from Silhouette® Romantic Suspense.*

Eight years ago Matt Shaffer had vanished out of Natalie Rothchild's life, leaving behind a one-line note tucked under a pillow that had grown cold: *I'm sorry, but this just isn't going to work.*

That was it. No explanation, no real indication of remorse. The note had been as clinical and compassionless as an eviction notice, which, in effect, it had been, Natalie thought as she navigated through the morning traffic. Matt had written the note to evict her from his life.

She'd spent the next two weeks crying, breaking down without warning as she walked down the street, or as she sat staring at a meal she couldn't bring herself to eat.

Candace, she remembered with a bittersweet pang, had tried to get her to go clubbing in order to get her to forget about Matt.

She'd turned her twin down, but she did get her act together. If Matt didn't think enough of their relationship to try to contact her, to try to make her understand why he'd changed so radically from lover to stranger, then to hell with him. He was dead to her, she resolved. And he'd remained that way.

Until twenty minutes ago.

The adrenaline in her veins kept mounting.

Natalie focused on her driving. Vegas in the daylight wasn't nearly as alluring, as magical and glitzy as it was after dark. Like an aging woman best seen in soft lighting, Vegas's imperfections were all visible in the daylight. Natalie supposed that was why people like her sister didn't like to get up until noon. They lived for the night.

Except that Candace could no longer do that.

The thought brought a fresh, sharp ache with it.

"Damn it, Candy, what a waste," Natalie murmured under her breath.

She pulled up before the Janus casino. One of the three valets currently on duty came to life and made a beeline for her vehicle.

"Welcome to the Janus," the young attendant said cheerfully as he opened her door with a flourish.

"We'll see," she replied solemnly.

As he pulled away with her car, Natalie looked up

at the casino's logo. Janus was the Roman god with two faces, one pointed toward the past, the other facing the future. It struck her as rather ironic, given what she was doing here, seeking out someone from her past in order to get answers so that the future could be settled.

The moment she entered the casino, the Vegas phenomenon took hold. It was like stepping into a world where time did not matter or even make an appearance. There was only a sense of "now."

Because in Natalie's experience she'd discovered that bartenders knew the inner workings of any establishment they worked for better than anyone else, she made her way to the first bar she saw within the casino.

The bartender in attendance was a gregarious man in his early forties. He had a quick, sexy smile, which was probably one of the main reasons he'd been hired. His name tag identified him as Kevin.

Moving to her end of the bar, Kevin asked, "What'll it be, pretty lady?"

"Information." She saw a dubious look cross his brow. To counter that, she took out her badge. Granted she wasn't here in an official capacity, but Kevin didn't need to know that. "Were you on duty last night?"

Kevin began to wipe the gleaming black surface of the bar. "You mean during the gala?"

"Yes."

The smile gracing his lips was a satisfied one.

Last night had obviously been profitable for him, she judged. "I caught an extra shift."

She took out Candace's photograph and carefully placed it on the bar. "Did you happen to see this woman there?"

The bartender glanced at the picture. Mild interest turned to recognition. "You mean Candace Rothchild? Yeah, she was here, loud and brassy as always. But not for long," he added, looking rather disappointed. There was always a circus when Candace was around, Natalie thought. "She and the boss had at it and then he had our head of security escort her out."

She latched onto the first part of his statement. "They argued? About what?"

He shook his head. "Couldn't tell you. Too far away for anything but body language," he confessed.

"And the head of security?" she asked.

"He got her to leave."

She leaned in over the bar. "Tell me about him."

"Don't know much," the bartender admitted. "Just that his name's Matt Shaffer. Boss flew him in from L.A., where he was head of security for Montgomery Enterprises."

There was no avoiding it, she thought darkly. She was going to have to talk to Matt. The thought left her cold. "Do you know where I can find him right now?"

Kevin glanced at his watch. "He should be in his office. On the second floor, toward the rear." He gave her the numbers of the rooms where the monitors that kept watch over the casino guests as they tried their luck against the house were located.

Taking out a twenty, she placed it on the bar. "Thanks for your help."

Kevin slipped the bill into his vest pocket. "Any time, lovely lady," he called after her. "Any time."

She debated going up the stairs, then decided on the elevator. The car that took her up to the second floor was empty. Natalie stepped out of the elevator, looked around to get her bearings and then walked toward the rear of the floor.

"Into the Valley of Death rode the six hundred," she silently recited, digging deep for a line from a poem by Tennyson. Wrapping her hand around a brass handle, she opened one of the glass doors and walked in.

The woman whose desk was closest to the door looked up. "You can't come in here. This is a restricted area."

Natalie already had her ID in her hand and held it up. "I'm looking for Matt Shaffer," she told the woman.

God, even saying his name made her mouth go dry. She was supposed to be over him, to have moved on with her life. What happened?

The woman began to answer her. "He's—"

"Right here."

The deep voice came from behind her. Natalie felt every single nerve ending go on tactical alert at the same moment that all the hairs at the back of her neck stood up. Eight years had passed, but she would have recognized his voice anywhere.

* * * * *

*Why did Matt Shaffer leave
heiress-turned-cop Natalie Rothchild?
What does he know about the death
of Natalie's twin sister?
Come and meet these two reunited lovers
and learn the secrets of the Rothchild family in
THE HEIRESS'S 2-WEEK AFFAIR
by USA TODAY bestselling author
Marie Ferrarella.
The first book in Silhouette® Romantic Suspense's
wildly romantic new continuity,
LOVE IN 60 SECONDS!
Available April 2009.*

You're invited to join our Tell Harlequin Reader Panel!

By joining our new reader panel you will:

- Receive Harlequin® books—they are FREE and yours to keep with no obligation to purchase anything!
- Participate in fun online surveys
- Exchange opinions and ideas with women just like you
- Have a say in our new book ideas and help us publish the best in women's fiction

In addition, you will have a chance to win great prizes and receive special gifts! See Web site for details. Some conditions apply. Space is limited.

To join, visit us at
www.TellHarlequin.com.

REQUEST YOUR FREE BOOKS!

2 FREE NOVELS PLUS 2 FREE GIFTS!

Passionate, Powerful, Provocative!

YES! Please send me 2 FREE Silhouette Desire® novels and my 2 FREE gifts (gifts are worth about $10). After receiving them, if I don't wish to receive any more books, I can return the shipping statement marked "cancel". If I don't cancel, I will receive 6 brand-new novels every month and be billed just $4.05 per book in the U.S. or $4.74 per book in Canada, plus 25¢ shipping and handling per book and applicable taxes, if any*. That's a savings of almost 15% off the cover price! I understand that accepting the 2 free books and gifts places me under no obligation to buy anything. I can always return a shipment and cancel at any time. Even if I never buy another book, the two free books and gifts are mine to keep forever.   225 SDN ERVX   326 SDN ERVM

Name	(PLEASE PRINT)	
Address		Apt. #
City	State/Prov.	Zip/Postal Code

Signature (if under 18, a parent or guardian must sign)

Mail to the Silhouette Reader Service:
IN U.S.A.: P.O. Box 1867, Buffalo, NY 14240-1867
IN CANADA: P.O. Box 609, Fort Erie, Ontario L2A 5X3

Not valid to current subscribers of Silhouette Desire books.

Want to try two free books from another line?
Call 1-800-873-8635 or visit www.morefreebooks.com.

* Terms and prices subject to change without notice. N.Y. residents add applicable sales tax. Canadian residents will be charged applicable provincial taxes and GST. Offer not valid in Quebec. This offer is limited to one order per household. All orders subject to approval. Credit or debit balances in a customer's account(s) may be offset by any other outstanding balance owed by or to the customer. Please allow 4 to 6 weeks for delivery. Offer available while quantities last.

Your Privacy: Silhouette Books is committed to protecting your privacy. Our Privacy Policy is available online at www.eHarlequin.com or upon request from the Reader Service. From time to time we make our lists of customers available to reputable third parties who may have a product or service of interest to you. If you would prefer we not share your name and address, please check here. ☐

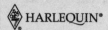

Harlequin® Historical
Historical Romantic Adventure!

THE RAKE'S
INHERITED COURTESAN
Ann Lethbridge

Christopher Evernden has been
assigned the unfortunate task of minding
Parisian courtesan Sylvia Boisette.
When Syliva sets off to find her father,
Christopher has no choice but to follow
and finds her kidnapped by an Irishman.
Once rescued, they finally succumb to
the temptation that has been brewing
between them. But can they see past the
limitations such a love can bring?

Available April 2009
wherever books are sold.

COMING NEXT MONTH
Available April 14, 2009

#1933 THE UNTAMED SHEIK—Tessa Radley
Man of the Month
Whisking a suspected temptress to his desert palace seems the
only way to stop her…until unexpected attraction flares and he
discovers she may not be what he thought after all.

#1934 BARGAINED INTO HER BOSS'S BED—Emilie Rose
The Hudsons of Beverly Hills
He'll do anything to get what he wants—including seduce his
assistant to keep her from quitting!

#1935 THE MORETTI SEDUCTION—Katherine Garbera
Moretti's Legacy
This charming tycoon has never heard the word *no*—until now.
Attracted to his business rival, he finds himself in a fierce battle
both in the boardroom...and the bedroom.

#1936 DAKOTA DADDY—Sara Orwig
Stetsons & CEOs
Determined to buy a ranch from his former lover and family rival,
he's shocked to discover he's a father! Now he'll stop at nothing
short of seduction to get his son.

**#1937 PRETEND MISTRESS, BONA FIDE BOSS—
Yvonne Lindsay**
Rogue Diamonds
His plan had been to proposition his secretary into being his
companion for the weekend. But he *didn't* plan on wanting more
than just a business relationship….

**#1938 THE HEIR'S SCANDALOUS AFFAIR—
Jennifer Lewis**
The Hardcastle Progeny
When the mysterious woman he spent a passionate night with
returns to tell him he may be a Hardcastle, he wonders what a
Hardcastle man should do to get her back in his bed.

SDCNMBPA0309